Switching Sides

www.barbarianspy.com

This book is copyright © habu 2017
habu asserts his right to be known as the author of this work.
Published by BarbarianSpy in 2017
Cover design © S Bush 2017
Cover images: manipulated: © hannamonika | illu
ISBN: E-Book: 978-1-925568-22-6
Paperback:978-1-925568-23-3
All rights reserved

BarbarianSpy
Toronto, Australia

Switching Sides

Habu

Table of Contents

Chapter One: Across the Line, Naples, Italy

"What is it?" I asked as Mario came close to me after we'd been shown to the table on the terrace of the Ciro' Restaurant overlooking the Marina Piccola—the little harbor—on the Italian island of Capri. Then, confused, I tensed, as he reached around me and pulled the tail of my sports shirt out of the waistband of my khakis. When he'd pulled it out all around, he proceeded to unbutton my shirt and let it flare out from my chest. I didn't have an undershirt under it. I just stood there, transfixed, with my mouth open, and let him do it.

"There. I've been wanting to do that ever since I picked you up at your hotel in Rome," he said. "You are supposed to be on vacation here, and you are a beautiful man. You should flaunt yourself. Has anyone ever told you you look like . . . like a slightly younger version of that American movie star . . . what's his name . . . ?"

"Yes, I've been told that a time or two," I said, not wanting to be told for the hundredth time that I looked like my father did when he was twenty years older than I was now.

That aside, I had wanted him to be this close to me ever since I'd seen what a hunk he was in the lobby of the small, yet elegant, hotel Peter had arranged for me in Rome, the Palazzo Manfredi, near the Coliseum. He had arranged the hotel just as he had arranged for Mario Farro to be my personal guide for the four days I was stopping here in transit to the Turkish coast. And yet I also was afraid to have him close to me. For a couple of years now I'd established that I wanted something radically different from my life in Cape May, back in the States, but I had done nothing about changing my lifestyle.

I was getting an inkling now that Peter had convinced me to make this stop in Rome and had made all of the arrangements, including Mario, to push me across that line.

"Sorry, this is all new to me," I muttered, giving him an embarrassed, shy smile as he backed off from me and sat in a chair across from me at the small table. We both sat sideways to the view of the small harbor and rock outcroppings rising from the Mediterranean. The harbor had been the playground, so Mario had told me as we walked up the stone stairs to the restaurant terrace, of the Roman emperors Augustus and Tiberius. The views from the terrace were stunning. If I had been less nervous, I'm sure I would have thoroughly enjoyed the view—and the day trip from Rome that so far had included the ruins of Pompeii in the morning and Naples, across the bay from where we now were on the island of Capri, in the early afternoon.

"I want to show you where there is a spectacular view of the sunset," Mario had said, and we'd taken the ferry over from Naples to Capri.

Mario wasn't dressed "uptight" as he had admonished me for doing. He wore worn jeans and sandals, without socks, and his gauzy white cotton shirt hung out of his jeans and was open to show a tanned and perfectly cut torso. A gold chain hung around his neck. That easily could be an Italian gigolo cliché, but it wasn't so with him. He was a beautiful young man, a good ten years younger than my thirty-seven, and in peak physical condition. He was neither skinny nor muscle bound. He had the look of a male model, including the curly black hair that also lightly patterned his chest, and a ruggedly handsome facial structure, with pale blue eyes and a sensual smile.

He had said more than once that I looked like a movie star. He had that look no less than I did, and we'd got appreciative stares from women and a certain kind of man throughout the day.

His English, although not perfect, was quite good enough. I knew absolutely no Italian. I'd been studying Turkish for the past four months, which didn't allow time for any other language study. Peter hadn't had a bit of trouble convincing me

8

that I'd need a guide dedicated totally to me for the stop in Italy. Of course that hadn't come up until Peter had convinced me that I needed a break between the States and Turkey and that the break might as well be in Rome.

So, I now thought, Peter had been scheming about this from the beginning. I didn't know whether to curse him or send him a thank-you telegram. I suppose that depended on just how far Mario's services went and if I could convince myself to go that far. He'd strongly hinted to me that he was gay when he'd first picked me up at the airport and had been effusive in saying how attractive I was. He hadn't asked about me, but he seemed to assume I was. I don't know if Peter had said I was farther down the road to that possibility than I was yet convinced I was. I dreamt about possibilities once I'd relocated to Turkey. I don't know what I would have thought if something was planned to happen before then.

"And, so, what do you think?" Mario asked after our drinks and a compartmented bowl with nuts, chips, and Greek olives had been plunked down on the table and the waitress had gone off to contend with a large party at the other end of the terrace. We were very much alone where we sat, watching the sun sink toward the horizon over the Mediterranean behind an outcropping of rocks rising out of the sea beyond the mouth of the ancient harbor. He pulled his chair around closer to beside me, "to get a better view of the sunset," he said rather loudly. I don't know if that was for my benefit or to be heard by the members of the group at the other end of the dining terrace. In any case the other group's attention was riveted on a small TV set featuring a soccer match.

"Naples is playing Palermo," Mario said, in way of an explanation. "That's why the restaurant isn't more crowded than it is," he added.

"Would you rather be watching the football match?" I asked.

"I'd rather be watching you," he said, with a smile. "So, what do you think of the view from here," he repeated, looking away from me now as if his other comment at been too forward.

"I think it's a sight to remember forever," I answered. "I'm glad you thought to bring me here."

"Ah, yes, ancient Marina Piccola," he said in a soft voice. "Quite the place to bring someone you are wooing—a real mood creator. Did you know that legend has this as where Ulysses was tempted by the sirens? And that men only slightly less god-like than Ulysses came here to couple? This is where the Roman emperor Tiberius brought his Sejanus and Emperor Augustus cavorted with his Marcus Agrippa."

"The emperor's lovers? To couple, you said."

"Yes, their male lovers—and not just young boys, which was the accepted rage then, but mature men. Coming here to fuck. So, what are you thinking about today?"

"Today has been great. You are an excellent tour guide. I feel like I've really experienced Pompeii and Naples. I'm looking forward to seeing Rome with you."

"You haven't really experienced Naples yet, Cliff," Mario said in a low voice. "We haven't established yet how extensively you want to make use of my services. This is not a simple sightseeing contract that was made with my service. I am available to you for very extensive personal services, as you wish."

I turned my eyes away from the sinking sun to look into Mario's eyes. My arm was resting on the top of the table and he moved a hand to the back of my forearm, touching me lightly there, brushing his fingers across my downy hair, making chills run up my spine. I had "gotten it" some time ago—in Pompeii, when he'd stayed so close to me, excusing it on the uneven cobble-stoned paving of the ancient streets, and I'd let my mind process what Peter was setting up for me here.

"I've never been with a man before," I said.

"I was told that probably was the case—but that you were here because you wanted to make major changes in your life—that you were going to Turkey to be a new man . . . a man's man. I was told you may need help switching sides in life. You are a very desirable man, Cliff. I have no qualms whatsoever in helping you across that threshold. But it's up to you to want it—to be open to the change now."

"Is this really all part of the services my friend engaged for my Italian stopover?"

"Yes. Do you mind? Do you want to avail yourself of all that's covered in the fees? I assure you, it would be a pleasure, not a chore for me."

"I don't know. It's something to think about. It will be quite late when we get back to Rome tonight. I doubt that we'll be . . . I just don't know."

"We don't have to go back to Rome tonight," Mario said. "I have booked a room at the Romeo Hotel in Naples. It's just across the road from the ferry port there. It's a very understanding hotel. The name of the hotel should make that clear." He laughed then, and I chuckled as well—nervously on my part, more easily on his. He certainly wasn't uncomfortable talking about possibilities. We were talking about him fucking me, and I'd never been with a man before, although I certainly had thought about it. Maybe it was because of this setting—the male-on-male playground of ancient Roman emperors—that made me think seriously about it now. Then again maybe it was because I'd been thinking about doing it for some time now, indeed, it had been at the foundation for me relocating to Turkey.

"It's completely up to you, of course," Mario continued, lifting his hand to brush a lock of my hair into place, "but I am available to you if you want to ease the way into why you are making these drastic changes in your life. The ferries will be running all evening. It's early yet in Italian time. We can be in Naples, in a room at the Romeo, within the hour." And then, almost as an afterthought, he said, "I can be as gentle or as forceful as you want. We can move from one to the other, as you please. The night is ours alone."

I turned my face toward the sun that was just now sinking below the horizon, creating a display of red, yellow, and purple streaks across the background of dark blue sky. The sinking of the sun. A glittering transition from one reality to another. The sensual toying of his fingers in the downy hair of my forearm was driving to me to distraction, and to combat that, I concentrated on the shifting scene before me with its changing patterns and intensity of light.

I must have been absorbed in the scene for some time because Mario finally spoke. "I've lost you, Cliff. What has taken you away from me?"

"Sorry," I answered, turning my head to look at him. The waning light from the sea, combined with the soft lights of the lanterns overhead on the framing of the terrace roof, composed of grape vines stretched across latticework, had brought a new beauty to Mario as well. Naples must have scored a goal, because the group across the terrace had erupted into a cheer. Their exuberance jolted me into a decision.

"I can't help myself," I responded to his remark on my reverie. "I was organizing what I see out there into a commercial photo shoot." I didn't want to baldly say yes to him—that, yes, I wanted him to fuck me. I'd have to make him understand without being blatant about it. I didn't want to be pathetic in my need for him.

"You are a photographer? That is your profession?"

"That's what I was before I married and opened a bed and breakfast with my wife—she was the decorator and chef— and I continued working on commercial photography on the side. Some fashion photography, some commercial layouts." I didn't want to admit that work wasn't a necessity for me. I had had the luxury of going for art for art's sake. My parents had been mainstays in Hollywood. I'd inherited a bundle and could pretty much live life where and as I liked—doing what I wanted. That was the issue that was taking me to Turkey, with this stopover. I wanted to be something radically different from what I had been to now.

"And what do you see out there?" he asked. He was leaning his head toward me, and it would be only a journey of a few inches for us to kiss. If he expected me to initiate that, though, he thought I was a much braver man than I was. "What's the focus of the photography out there? The rock formations outside the harbor entrance?"

"No," I said, and smiled. "The rocks and sunset provide an arresting background, but the focus is that small sailing boat coming into the harbor and the young man hiking the sail to pull the boat into the safety of the port. The young man and the boat, working together to one end they both need."

"Ah, yes, I see him now. He's a beautiful young man. I can see why a discerning eye would focus on him in this setting. Do you find him sexy . . . sensual?"

"Yes," I answered honestly. "I see both the young man and the boat as sexy—the two of them moving together, working together toward a fulfillment." I wanted Mario to understand that I was giving him a yes. We didn't speak for a few minutes as we watched the young man, outfitted only in a skimpy bathing suit bring the small sailboat onto the sand below the terrace, pull it up above the tide line, give it a hug that almost screamed what I was trying to say to Mario, and pad up a stone staircase, taking him away from us and into what now had become a mere hint of display of color on the horizon.

"And you see him—and his interaction with the boat—as an attractive subject of a photograph?"

"Yes," I said, and followed up with a revealing honesty that I had no idea I would admit. "It's what much of my photography is now. Young men—and their interactions."

"Nudes?" Mario asked, probing.

"Yes," I admitted. "I have a subscription service of a select clientele interested in such photos."

"You've complimented me. Would you desire to photograph me nude?"

"Yes," I said, in a breathy voice.

"Alone, or with another man?"

"Both."

"That could be arranged," he whispered and then leaned farther into me and took my lips with his. He tasted of the rich and heady Tuscan Cabernet Franc he'd ordered for us. His kiss was light at first, then a few brief seconds of promised fire, his tongue pressing between my lips, before receding again into a lingering brushing of lips. I gave him no resistance. I was hard, wanting him. But he pulled away from me and we both turned our eyes to the dying sunset.

It was Mario who broke the silence. "Cliff? What do you want from me? I am yours to command; you can have

13

whatever you prefer. I'm told you will probably be a top, but we can explore that. I am versatile; I can help guide you to be whatever you want to be. It's already been paid for. The hotel has been booked."

He had understood my "yes."

* * * *

I will be eternally grateful to Mario—and to Peter, who undoubtedly paid a fortune on my behalf—for initiating me as gently but also as fully as he was being paid to do—and did so as if he wanted to do it, that he wasn't being paid to do it.

He started on the ferry, finding a secluded spot on the upper deck for us, where we could pretend we were watching the departing Isle of Capri and waning light of the sunset and then the approaching waterfront of Naples in its northern curve or, over the south curve of the bay the still-active volcano, Vesuvius. We sat on a wooden-backed bench, with empty benches all around us, huddled close together for all intents and purposes for protection from the wind whipping across the ferry as it steamed to the distant ferry port. In fact, though, we stole kisses when we thought we weren't being observed and Mario's hands were busy in under my open sports shirt, along the surface of my khaki slacks, which somehow became unbuckled and unzipped in the enclosed space between our bench and the one in front of us.

There were one or two other sets of couples on the upper deck, but since they were up here to be at least as intimate as we were being, we were accorded enough privacy for kisses and more. I was aware that we weren't fooling anyone, but it also became clear to me why Peter had suggested this stop in Italy. No one appeared to be outraged that two men were making out on the ferry. Most of them were making out as well and not concerned with passing judgments. Italy seemed to be a paradise that valued sexual expression over gender identification, which caught me by surprise coming from a heavily Catholic country.

I received my first hand job from a man on that ferry, coming embarrassingly quickly and being overwhelmed in the momentous event—certainly for me, if not for Mario. He had coaxed me to do the same for him, but I'd not gone farther than running my hand tentatively through his chest hair a couple of times and, once he took my hand and placed it there, cupping his genitals through the material of his shorts as he was jacking me off, before I came and, in embarrassment, turned from him, folded myself back into my fly, zipped myself up, and pretended to be engrossed in examining the outline of Mount Vesuvius.

"Sorry," I muttered in embarrassment. "I should have been willing to do for you what you did for me."

"No matter," he'd answered smoothly. "I know it's all knew to you. You will be able to be freer in private."

In truth, he had put my senses into as much turmoil as the cauldron of any volcano. I'd done it—taken the first step. The first time I'd kissed a man—or let a man kiss me, rather, and hadn't pulled away from that. And the first time I'd let a man wrap his hand around my cock, me becoming hard under his touch, and stroke me off and made me come for him. I'd never been sure before—whether I really could harden for a man and come for him. Now I knew.

And now I knew I wanted him to do it again—that I wanted to do it for Mario too. And more, maybe more. But he was right about privacy being a need for me to be that intimate—at least for now.

Mario was great with my nervousness and my turning away. He put his arm around me, whispered how everything was fine and we'd go step by step—and that it was natural that I would have come so quickly but still be reluctant about other matters.

I was a basket case before we'd gotten to the Romeo Hotel, and it's a good thing it was just across a promenade street from the ferry port. And it was even better that the man—thank god it was a man—at the reception desk acted like nothing was more natural than two men checking into one room at the hotel with nothing more than small backpacks. Mario had told me to bring a clean shirt and underwear as we would be going on the water and I might need dry clothes. The reception clerk even smoothly came up with two toiletry kits as

15

if these went to everyone checking in. Mario had told me that the hotel would be no problem—that we were in the middle of the Chiaia gay district of the city—and he had been right. Mario was taking care of everything.

It wasn't lost on me that the toiletry kits included packets of condoms.

Mario even at just the right moment turned into the submissive, maneuvering me to fuck him first before he, in turn, fucked me, saying I should experience both options before determining my natural nature and that if I preferred top, which he assumed I would, I would enjoy it more by having some idea of what my partner was experiencing.

Throwing our backpacks and new toiletry kits aside on the foot of the bed when we entered the room, we went directly to the bed ourselves. It was a king-sized bed, obviously the most important—and most used—piece of furniture in the room. Mario didn't give me time to hyperventilate over what we were doing. He quickly had us stretched out together. As we went down he pulled his shirt off his back and then mine as well. I was in his embrace and we were kissing immediately. And he had his hands all over me. He unbuckled and unzipped me again as we were kissing. And he did that for himself as well. He probably knew I would need more build-up to doing that than he wanted to give him in his steamroll to sex that went beyond the kissing and hand job on the ferry.

He stroked me for a while and moved my hand to his cock. The first time I'd done that with a man, but he had me in the moment and in heat and he wasn't giving me time or space to think about what we were doing. After pulling out of our kiss and running his tongue across my lips to assure himself that I would open my mouth to him if he wanted a deeper kiss, he moved his face down my throat and to my chest, working my nipples to the point of me recognizing that they were an arousal zone for me. I moaned for him and held his head to me with a hand.

He lifted his head and whispered, "I'm going to do everything to you."

"Yes, yes," I answered with a groan. Periodically he stopped and asserted that we were moving on to more, and each time I whispered "yes." This was my opportunity to experience all I'd dreamed about, all I'd seen being done between men across the fence at my B&B in Cape May. A fulfillment of my fantasies. I couldn't let this go. Mario was young and beautiful and hard bodied. And he was whispering of the pleasures we were going to experience together.

I lost my shoes and khakis and socks and he smoothly disrobed as well. My initial embarrassment and worry about being naked with him was ended by his exclamations of how toned I was for my age and how well endowed I was—that he was pleased that I was hard for him. That he couldn't wait for me to be inside him.

Then he took me in his mouth—the first time a man had sucked my cock—and I suddenly was busy working hard not to explode as prematurely as I had down in his hand on the ferry.

He took his mouth off my cock, looked up at me, and said. "You say you photograph young men. Do you photograph them servicing your cock?"

"I've never had a man sucking me before," I answered, my voice shaking.

"Your camera is just there," he said. "Use it."

I did, and I think having a camera to point down the line of my torso to catch what he was doing with my cock in his mouth helped me control myself. I think otherwise I would have come almost immediately.

He was professional. He could sense when I was tensing and he backed off until I had calmed down. But he didn't give up on me, and later, when he moved his body around, hovering over mine, and his hard cock was there, the bulb pressing at my lips, I did the natural move and opened to him. He was restrained, giving me just a few inches. He took the camera from me, held it in one hand, while supporting himself over me with the other arm, and it was my turn being photographed sucking cock.

We'd been on the move all day. He tasted salty and tangy. The smooth, spongy texture of his glans contrasted with the rough, hard-as-steel of his shaft as I moved my mouth farther down the sides of his cock, taking more of him inside

17

me. He put the camera to the side to concentrate fully on me, and then he was way ahead of me, taking nearly all of my cock with each down stroke. I pressed my tongue into his piss slit as he had done with mine, and he rewarded me with a deep moan, just as I had done when he had tongued my slit.

I warned him I couldn't take much more, and he murmured, "That will come in time," and turned on me, rising up on his knees, planted on either side of my thighs, as he turned me on my back, looking up at his magnificent, hard torso. He picked up the camera and took a photo of my face in deep want. The camera went to our pelvises, capturing his hand wrapped around our two cocks, frotting them.

I moaned again, as he put the camera aside and reached for one of the toiletry kits, which, as I'd already noticed, contained a small bottle of lube and a couple of condom packets along with the usual toothbrush, toothpaste, and disposable shaving supplies.

I trembled as he opened a packet and unrolled a condom on my hard and throbbing cock, applied lube to the shaft and to his ass, and then saddled himself on my pelvis, impaled himself a couple of inches to obtain purchase, palmed my pecs, looked dreamily down into my eyes, and fucked himself on my shaft.

Again, I came embarrassingly quickly and again he assured me that this was natural for the first time and that I'd gain greater control through repetition.

I had fucked my first man.

"Now me. The pain will melt into pleasure, but let me know if it gets too much," he whispered as he crowned himself with another condom, turned me on my side, with him stretched behind me, and ran an arm under my waist, palming my lower belly and jutting my buttocks back and up. I gulped as I felt his bulb inside my rim. He placed his free hand under my knee and lifted my leg.

I gasped and tried not to cry out as he slowly entered me. It was almost more than I could bear, but bear it I did, and then it wasn't more than I could take and I was taking him as he slow stroked me. I don't think he went deep, but it felt like he was fucking me with a telephone pole.

"Memorializing your first time," I heard him murmur, and I looked around to see that he had the camera again and that it was trained on his cock moving in my ass. I came again before he did, with him giving a small laugh and whisper, "Good, good. Yes, you want to go with men." And then he tensed and jerked, and it was done. I'd been fucked by my first man.

He rode my cock again after a short break, complimenting me on my fast reload. This time it was freer and he bounced more—and urged me to grab his waist and thrust more, which I did—and enjoyed it thoroughly. I held the camera this time and fired off photos of him riding me. I was finding that including the camera in the sex play helped me manage my arousal.

"In a bit we'll clean up and go out on the town. You must be starving," he said. He was still on top of me, me flaccid inside him, and he leaning over and kissing me on the mouth and the throat and the nipples. At that moment what I was starving for was to move him on his back and take control in fucking him. But that was to come.

We ate on the terrace beside the hotel's pool, not being dressed for its four-star restaurant, and then we walked for a few blocks to the Ghetto Crime Bar, where we ogled and were ogled. We both were propositioned, but Mario said the pickings were better at another bar—a cruising club not far away.

"The pickings?" I asked.

"No reason just to wade. It's all in tonight. Tonight we buy you a young lay. Tomorrow night we find someone as nice who wants to go to the hotel with you just because he wants you to lay him."

I hyperventilated, but I didn't say no or second guess what Mario wanted to do.

The cruising club was the Depot Napoli. There were many young men on offer. I picked a young Greek out and we took him back to the Romeo. He was amenable to being photographed for extra money. After I took some solo nude poses of him, Mario fucked him as I watched, sitting in a chair by the bed and pointing the camera. Then, still gaping open

19

from Mario fucking him missionary style on the bed, the Italian stud gathered him up, still saddled, and carried him—Nick, he'd said—over to me. Mario put him on my cock, facing me, as I sat there, luckily having rolled a rubber on earlier at Mario's command. Mario took a turn with the camera. Nick rode me, his arms around my neck, his lips on mine for a while, until he jerked his mouth off mine, gave a little cry, and threw his head back. Mario was behind him. I felt Mario's cock working its way into the Greek's passage above mine. Mario grabbed Nick's waist and stroked his ass, rubbing along my stationary shaft inside the passage.

My first night with a man, and already I had done a DP of a man with another man.

We returned to Rome the next day, and my sex education continued to expand and deepen as Mario introduced me to the gay district of Rome near my hotel, the Palazzo Manfredi. Surmising—correctly—that I liked topping the best, Mario didn't fuck me again, but I fucked him in a variety of positions he introduced me to. Our club crawls and experiences doing the same things each night were as exhausting as they were educational.

When I boarded a plane at the Rome airport, waving good-bye to my accommodating guide, I was tired, drained, and felt like there was electricity coursing through my body. I had been indoctrinated well. I would have to send a thank-you card to Peter, in Cape May, knowing that this was his doing—and at his considerable expense. I also had a couple of full cartridges of photos to pass on to my service subscribers.

But the one thing I didn't feel was fully satisfied, fulfilled. I was thirty-seven. I didn't see myself sustaining a cruising lifestyle for any length of time. Indeed, Mario's program had almost killed me. There was something else that was missing. I couldn't put my finger on it—something I had expected switching sides would bring to me that I'd seen in the gay community in Cape May—a community that would have welcomed me, I'm sure, if I'd been ready for it, but I wasn't. Something else I was seeking other than this wanton orgy I'd experienced in Rome.

Still, there was no shyness left for me. There was not much I hadn't done for the first time—and the second time—or would not understand how to do the next time. There certainly wasn't more I could do that wasn't memorialized in film.

~

Chapter Two: Before That, Cape May, New Jersey

This move to switching sides was a long process in coming, and it was gradual enough that I didn't see the inevitability of it for a long time. I certainly was slow in seeing that it was what I wanted. I fought it for years—but not so consciously that I realized for some time that it even was a fight. I thought it was something just there as a choice I wasn't making because I wouldn't like the consequences. My life was fine without complete sexual satisfaction—or so I thought for the longest time.

The inkling that I was aroused by men—more so than by women, who, I'll acknowledge, I didn't have much trouble getting it up for as well—came in the years that I transitioned in New York from commercial ad photography of all varieties to fashion photography, first of women models and then, increasingly, of men as well. Slowly, nude photography drifted into this as an aside and, because it paid well and aroused me, I also photographed, tastefully posed, of course, sex acts and couplings for private collections. Initially these were of heterosexual couples, but they drifted into poses between women. Increasingly these became couplings between men. If I was aware that the solo and coupled poses of men aroused me more than others, I sublimated that. I managed to put that in the background for as long as I worked in New York. And, eventually, because there was a market for it, I was photographing only men.

I never, in New York, though, advanced to including myself in the photo shoots. I may have masturbated to copies of the photos later, but I'd done that with the photos of heterosexual couplings as well, and when I was working I was concentrating on the sensuality of the poses and acts themselves rather than the genders—or so I told myself.

That was where I met Caroline. She was a model who was really easy on the eyes and who had a husky southern accent—she was from a wealthy family in Charleston, South Carolina—that sent chills up my spine. She was somewhat of a Martha Stewart type—she had a highly successful southern-style interior design and culinary business—and had entered modeling as well by being her own spokesperson in commercial ad layouts and being encouraged to go from there into fashion modeling on the side. The modeling enhanced her home accents consulting business.

I first photographed her for the commercial layouts and then moved with her into the fashion model photography and then, at her invitation, into the more intimate poses. She let me know in no uncertain terms that she was available to me, and we started sleeping together somewhere along that route. She wasn't the only photographic subject I slept with, but they were all women. No matter how, eventually, I found I was aroused by men as well, I was so far into denial that I only slept with women during my years working in New York.

Caroline was the only one from that period of my life who I married as well, and, both of us seeking a change in our lives, we moved out of New York into a new, shared life. We bought a B&B in the long-time seaside resort town of Cape May, New Jersey, where I took on restoring an old six-bedroom Victorian mansion on Decatur Street, three blocks off the beachfront. I handled the management responsibilities, and Caroline decorated it, including furnishings and décor that was for sale, and took on the breakfast duties.

Cape May is a pretty gay town. The Realtor who sold us the Decatur Street Inn, Michael Beard, was gay—and made that obvious in catering to me more than Caroline while we were shopping for a house we could turn into a B&B. The local travel agent, Peter Philips, we connected with to help link the B&B with tourists was gay. He obviously was a couple with his assistant, Ergon Seljek. Even the couple who ran the B&B next to the one we opened, Alex Renard and Sean Temple, of Gaylords Inn, were gay—and they openly ran their small hotel as a gay-insistent facility, and almost to the point, maybe beyond the point, of being a gay bordello. This wasn't a change from the commercial art community I was involved in in New York City, but it was more pronounced here because it was an obvious subset of the Cape May community, and it was only here that I was welcomed into this circle and treated like one of them.

I was treated like one of them despite not having engaged in homosexual relations the whole time I lived in Cape May—or before that for that matter. But I obviously had progressed to the point that they were comfortable about my fundamental interests even if I wasn't. But even in Cape May it was nearly two years before Peter Philips slapped me in the face with reality and moved the issue to the front of my consciousness.

"I'm not telling you this because I want to have sex with you, Cliff," he'd said as we were sitting at the Avalon Coffee House on nearby Gurney Street, sipping beer and watching the people on the Cape May beach—the young men in their skimpy Speedos mostly. Peter was assessing them and I wasn't being committal. But I was ogling them as much as Peter was. "Unless I'm quite mistaken, you are a top just as I am, and so you're not for me. But you are aching for it, I think. And it's time for you to admit that."

Perhaps I'd had too much beer, because I opened up to him then. Life hadn't been good with Caroline for some months. We still dutifully had sex twice a week, but it seemed to be on a routine schedule now and to be more a form of physical exercise than ecstasy. Where once we'd readily agreed to any ideas the other had on running the B&B, we now both seemed to go out of our way to object to what the other one suggested. She didn't come out and accuse me of fucking men, but she'd stumbled on my photography "special" portfolios and seen how extensive they were, she knew I was comfortable with the likes of Peter and Ergon and Alex and Sean, and she dropped a jab or two here and there. In turn, I suspected she was having it off with a local restaurateur. We both realized, I'm sure, that we were headed toward a split, and our attitudes toward the B&B business now seemed more like holding our

24

breaths and managing a holding action rather than thinking of building what we had into the future.

I told Peter about what weighed most on my mind. I told him of my visits to our attic and to the circular window overlooking the terrace and pool of the neighboring property, the extremely gay-male-friendly Gaylords Inn owned and run by Alex Renard and Sean Temple. The place was a tourist B&B, yes, but it went beyond welcoming gay male couples to providing paying guests with company, if they so wished and paid for it. I could only imagine what went on inside the blue Victorian mansion trimmed in pink. But out at the pool, everything happened, from full-body massage by a male masseur in the open-sided pool house to nude sunbathing and swimming . . . and sex . . . in the pool area—not only by couples but in multiple groups too. The proprietors, both hunks, helped provide the extra services.

That didn't put me off either Alex or Sean. Like Caroline, they mixed antiques in with their B&B décor that was for sale. If someone was looking for something in particular that they didn't have, they were quick to send them over to us. Also, if someone booked in their B&B who hadn't expected it to be exclusively for gay males, Sean would redirect them to us. Alex was the chef and he and Caroline got on famously and exchanged breakfast recipes. Sean was the manager, and if it hadn't been for his help with tips on running a B&B, I don't know how the Decatur Street Inn would have managed to stay in the black our first year.

For all that I could see, Alex and Sean were a happily married couple and balanced each other. That's more than I could say for Caroline and me, and I admit that I envied them. The truth was, though, that I envied them their setup over there next door even more. I didn't declare my interests to them—I admit to fantasizing about the tall, redheaded, burly, French-Canadian-extraction Alex, who obviously was the top of the couple, Sean being a breezy, laid-back California surfer type. Indeed, even to that point I was avoiding declaring it to myself. What I fantasized, though, was being Alex, with Sean submissive to my desires. But I think they knew I was attracted to them and they treated me like family. Being in denial didn't prevent me from going to the attic whenever I could and watching the activity in the pool area of the B&B next door.

"I have fought the urge to take my camera with me and to photograph the young men next door and what they were doing," I told Peter. "I still have the contact information for the private clients I photographed young men for in New York. They still would pay well, I know. But the men I photographed in New York were aware of what I was doing—and why—and they were paid well and signed releases. It would have been an unforgivable intrusion on Alex and Sean and their guests to photograph them. I could rationalized that the photos were just for me, I suppose, but . . ."

"But you still don't want to admit that you are aroused by this—seeing men with men live and in photographs."

"Yes, I suppose."

"Caroline? Caroline doesn't—?"

"No, she doesn't know. Not that she cares anymore. I think our time together is drawing to a close, Peter."

"That's a shame," he said. "But if the marriage is on the way out, there's no reason not to be moving toward where we both know you want to go. You're a handsome man, Cliff, and easy to be with. You deserve to turn to your natural inclinations."

"I don't know. I—"

"Come back to my place with me. Now, Cliff."

"Whoa. I'm not anywhere ready to—"

"No, not to have sex. I don't think it would work with the two of us anyway. I'm sure you have the same inclinations that I do. And, no, I'm not willing to share Ergon with you. We are happily paired. But you are a professional photographer, aren't you?"

"Yes."

"And you say you've photographed naked men."

"Yes."

"And in pairs, fucking."

"When they've wanted to go to that end. I've always gotten my shots and left them to it if that's what they wanted to do."

"And later? Did you get yourself off later, wanting at the core of you to have been included in their coupling?"

I paused to think about that, although it was more whether I wanted to admit to it than that I hadn't thought about it before. "Yes, maybe, I guess," was the best I could come up with.

"Ergon would like to have such photographs done—of us. I'll pay you the going rate. And it will give you an opportunity to check out just how comfortable you are with men being with men. If, in the process, you find you want to be involved, you can be—only if you want . . . no pressure. You have to start somewhere. What's important is getting started."

I agreed to it, and knowing the offer was there to participate at any point I was moved to do so probably was what starting me down the road to switching sides.

They were an attractive couple, even in their lovemaking . . . especially in their lovemaking, as there was an obvious passion and sense of being lost to each other in them. They were both beautiful. Although Peter was in his forties, he kept himself in tip-top condition. He was of sturdy English ancestry and was meaty, but, on him, it was well distributed and conveyed a sense of vitality. His blondness contrasted with Ergon's darkness and Mediterranean complexion. He was shorter than Peter and lithe. Peter had met him while on one of those familiarization trips travel agents took to be able to talk of locations knowledgably with their clients. He met Ergon on a beach on the Turkish coast and brought him home.

"Turkish men are especially sensual—openly and unapologetically sexy," Peter said. That thought stuck with me.

I photographed them for nearly an hour as they moved from kissing, fully clothed, to stripping each other down, moving into sixty-nine positions, and, eventually, Ergon lying stretched out on his belly, with Peter covering him close from above, holding the younger, smaller man in an embrace, and fucking him deep. The point of penetration didn't show well in my photographs, which I would airbrush when I developed them to give them an extra sense of artiness and romance, but it was clear that both men were in ecstasy from what they were giving to and taking from each other.

It was so sensual—far more sensual than any other scene I had photographed, as I hadn't photographed beyond the climax before, the principle being that the sex I was photographing was ostensibly simulated to give it the pretense of being art rather than pornography.

I stayed with them there, with Peter and Ergon, that afternoon, though, through the climax to the cool down, and in what I suppose could technically be called including myself in their sexual encounter, I unzipped myself and brought myself to a climax too even as I continued snapping off photos.

"You stayed. And you finished with us," Peter said when they were done, Ergo had padded off to the shower, and Peter had wrapped a robe around his body and lit up a cigarette.

"Yes, I'm sorry," I said. "I've never done that before. I should have left."

"But you don't regret having stayed, do you?" he asked.

"No, I don't regret it," I answered truthfully.

"We'll have to develop on that," he said. "You won't be truly satisfied until you've tried it all. I don't really mind if you do Ergon as long as I am there to share him with you."

I didn't answer him. I was afraid he probably was right, but I didn't want to let that devil out of the sack—at least not until I had resolved my relationship with Caroline.

A couple of days later Peter laid temptation before me. He called me from Gaylords Inn next door, saying that there was something over there he wanted help with. When I got there, he was conversing with Alex and Sean.

"I've been telling Alex and Sean about the photo shoot you did with Ergon and me," he said. "And they would like such a portfolio done on them—and they'd like to offer photo shoots as services for their guests."

"I don't know," I started to say, but then I thought, why the hell not? So, that fall and winter I stole next door with my cameras when my services were called upon. I didn't tell Caroline what I was doing, and she didn't ask. Increasingly she was spending time with her restaurateur, and we now were

28

speaking openly about life beyond our marriage. Our sticking point was that we both had personal equity in and attachment to the B&B. We just didn't want to remain business partners after divorcing. I guess, as well, both of us being competitive business people, we didn't want to admit to a failure in any endeavor we'd entered.

In one other regard, Peter's plans didn't pan out for me either. As aroused I was by the men I photographed at Gaylords Inn, I couldn't bring myself, while I still was in a partnership in any way with Caroline, to go beyond getting myself off by myself when I was photographing a sex coupling.

I agreed with Peter that I was moving in the direction of greater sexual experience with another man—and that I wanted to move in that direction—but I just couldn't bring myself to go there.

* * * *

"What you need then, after you have turned the Decatur Street Inn over to Caroline," Peter said one early spring morning as we sat and drank coffee in the Avalon Café, "is a total break."

"I don't know about a total break," I answered. "I enjoyed owning a B&B." By the end of that week, though, I wouldn't have an ownership stake in the Decatur Street Inn. Our divorce was coming through and I'd finally given in to giving up the B&B. Caroline's family had plenty of money. They could buy me out; I had the money too and had offered to buy Caroline out but she'd refused—out of spite, I thought. So, that was that. I'd been looking at other properties in Cape May, but Peter was finally getting through to me. I couldn't stay in Cape May and get on with a new life, what Peter kept calling "switching sides." If I couldn't stay for any other reason, it was because Caroline seemed determined to stay and run the B&B. Being in the same town with her would make life miserable for both of us.

"I don't know where else I could go," I said.

"As far from here as possible," Peter answered. "A total break, at least for now. A chance to start with a clean

29

slate, a life that's totally different from the one you have here. Tell me," he went on, "I've seen you ogling Ergon. He turns you on, doesn't he?—his dark hair and complexion, his happy disposition, his sensuality. You needn't be coy with me. If he were free of me—which he isn't, mind you; this is all hypothetical—would he be a man you would like to fuck?"

"Yes, of course. And more," I said. "You and he are more than sex partners—you are life partners too. I wouldn't think of going after him, but, yes, I find him very arousing."

"Well, there are more like him where he came from, and the Turkish coast is a tourist haven. I'm sure Turkey would benefit from another small seaside hotel there. And there are plenty of young men there, like Ergon, who would salivate over a hunky American like you. You're aging well, Cliff. Did anyone ever tell you you are the spitting image of that movie star—?"

"Yes, I think you've said that a dozen times yourself, Peter," I said, cutting him off from the overfamiliar comparison.

Thus it was that we started cruising the Internet, looking for buildings on the Turkish coast that could be renovated into a small B&B. The search narrowed on the coast around Kusadasi, the port city that served the popular tourist destination of the ruins of the biblical city of Ephesus. The area was ideal for my purposes, or so Peter insisted.

Peter didn't let me catch my breath once I'd said that maybe I was interested. He did all of the planning of buying that property and two others nearby, one at the seaside and one in the mountains, via the Internet and all of my travel arrangements, including a short stop in Rome, where I was to find that he had other plans for me as well.

"Who the hell buys a stone pile needing renovation that's located in a far away country they've never even visited?" I asked.

"You do. The new you does," Peter answered. "The man who is going to totally change his lifestyle. The man who is going to switch sides and start to have a life—to live life to its fullest."

~

30

Chapter Three: Rising from the Rubble

From Rome I sailed east across the Mediterranean on a small merchant ship that took on a limited number of passengers. In booking the voyage, my travel agent, Peter Phillips, had said that these vessels plying the inner seas of Europe were every bit as comfortable and accommodating as the cruise lines were—and a good bit cheaper. He proved to be right about that, and I'm glad he'd remembered how little I liked to fly and avoided it whenever possible. He also made side remarks about the male-male sex that could be easily found among fit sailors on these vessels, but I was so worn out in that department from Rome that I, initially, at least, didn't give that a thought for two days outbound from Italy.

What the slower progress across the Mediterranean did for me was that it gave me time to think. The last six months had been such a whirlwind of momentous decisions and hurried planning that I hadn't had time to think about what I was doing, and every time I paused for a breath and to weigh my options, Peter was there with his own form of answers and I just gave in to them. Here, on the freighter, I had all the time in the world to review what I was sailing into and the new lifestyle I was being propelled into.

Peter had pumped me for what I wanted to do and where I wanted to do it in the wake of my split from Caroline.

"I really do enjoy running the B&B and it allows me time for my photography," I'd answered.

"So, do you want to remain partners with Caroline in the Decatur Inn and move into a place of your own? Ergon and I have a small guest house you could rent until you found someplace else."

"Continuing as Caroline's partner in the B&B isn't an option. she's buying me out," I answered. "And I don't think I want to stay in Cape May. I think it's best to put a great deal of distance between Caroline and me."

"Ergon and I were sort of hoping you'd stay around. But if you want to go someplace else, I can help you get there. Were you thinking of any place in particular?"

"Somewhere Mediterranean. Greece or Turkey, maybe. Someplace on the coast." The answer had surprised me as much as it surprised Peter. I hadn't, in fact, thought about it. That just came out. But then I'd remembered that Peter once told me that there were other men in Turkey like Ergon— young and good-looking and submissive. Once the idea had been voiced, I realized I had been interested in the eastern Mediterranean for some time. Caroline and I had taken a vacation there a few years earlier, and I'd been taken with the region—and with the young sun worshippers I had seen there—young people of both sexes and with very good bodies. I had thought at the time how much I'd like to photograph them. "But I want to do more than just pursue photography," I continued. "And I have money to invest in something that will make money for me."

"Greece and Turkey—especially the coasts—are tourist havens," Peter said. "We'd have to get you documented, but foreigners can own small businesses like boutique hotels, at least in Turkey."

"So I could continue with the B&B idea?" I said. "I'd like something rustic, a stone village house maybe, one that I could have renovated to serve the small hotel purpose well. But I wouldn't know how—"

"Real estate worldwide is sold on the Internet these days," Peter said. "We can find just what you want."

"And buy it sight unseen?" I'd asked incredulously.

"Sight unseen," he answered. "I can help make sure you aren't taken, though. I've told you you need to go the whole way—to switch sides completely. Taking risks like this are what you need to start doing."

And so, as Peter sat with me at the computer, I bought three properties in and near Kusadasi, Turkey, via the Internet.

Two extremely cheap houses: one north of Kusadasi, in the quaint coastal village of Bayraklidede, was in need of total renovation but attracted me as a place for me to live; and a second one, in the mountainous area inland from Kusadasi, would, I thought, make a great mountain retreat and short-term rental property—once it no longer wasn't a mere gutted stone shell. The third property, larger and in the old town of Kusadasi itself, needed updating, but I could live there while it was being turned into an eight-bedroom, luxury guest house. That would be my answer to a B&B to run.

And why Kusadasi? It not only was on the Turkish resort coast but it also was the cruise tour port town giving access to the biblically significant ruined city of Ephesus, which attracted tens of thousands of tourists every year. The major city of Izmir, whose inhabitants used the Kusadasi region for a retreat, lay just sixty miles to the southeast. Caroline and I had gone through Kusadasi to visit Ephesus a few years earlier, and I'd remembered how we had remarked that this would be a great, cheap place to cash in on the tourist trade if we wanted to go international with our B&B operations. It seemed only natural that this, a world away from Caroline and Cape May and my former lifestyle, would be where I would come to start a new life.

That part of what I thought about as my freighter with its passenger section steamed east across the Mediterranean became solidified in my mind. Once again taking charge where I had indecision or lacked knowledge, Peter had hooked me up with a Kusadasi lawyer and Realtor, Cemil Teke, not only to smooth me through the process of a foreign investor in Turkey but also through the renovation process on my three new properties.

"He's gay—flamboyantly so. I met him at an international Realtor's conference," Peter had said. "You won't be attracted to him or he to you for very long beyond his initiation fee, but he'll help you in switching sides as well as in all of your setup needs. Normally, you'd have to watch him like a hawk, but we went cruising together and have an understanding, so I think he will deal with you as he would

33

with me. You'll need someone like him in Turkey. They are great people, but they are sharp in business."

"What do you mean by 'beyond his initiation fee'?" I asked, "and 'for very long'?"

"Ah, you caught that. It shouldn't be a big deal by the time you get to Turkey. You've indicated you're interested in trying both ways although you probably want to be dominant. Teke doesn't work with anyone he hasn't dominated first. After that, there's rarely anything he'll want from you. His primary interests are in someone much younger than either you or me."

"Dominated?"

"Fucked. As a top."

"And you? Did he dominate you?"

"Yes. He fucked the stuffing out of me. And then he lost interest and introduced me to Ergon."

I didn't ask questions about Peter and Teke beyond this and he didn't volunteer any more information.

When Cemil Teke's sexual interests came into my mind, which, I gather, involved interests in those of less than legal age, even in Turkey, the other thoughts I struggled with during my voyage to Turkey came up. The depths to which I had delved into sexual activity in Rome had aroused me, but they had also frightened me. How much I enjoyed bedding young men and what I had learned in Rome to do in doing so disturbed me. Was I moving too deep into the world too fast? I couldn't help but think that it easily could control me and make me into something I didn't want to be. Did I really want to make a switch, or was it just my relationship with Caroline having gone south that made me think I was off women?

It was Emilee, a passenger on the freighter whose last name I didn't learn until we disembarked, who made me question my radical decision of a change in lifestyle. She was everything in a woman that Caroline wasn't—petite, dark, shy, and totally feminine and sensual. When we encountered each other at meals and in passing on deck, she would give me looks that sent a chill up my spine and caused my cock to harden. I couldn't tell if she was coming on to me or just naturally sexually charged. And it didn't matter which—she turned me on when I was in the process of concluding that women didn't do that for me.

The kicker was that the young man she was with, a Turk named Talal, did the same for me. And when I caught them together in a remote area of the deck in the middle of the night when I couldn't sleep and had left my cabin to go out to the rail to try to let the action of the waves lull me into a stupor, I found that I didn't really know which of them I wanted more.

They both were naked, their clothes strewn on the deck around the lounge chair they were writhing on. Talal was on his back on the chair, with Emilee saddled on his cock, her head bent over, her eyes locked on his, and her luxuriant auburn hair cascading down onto her arms and back. She was palming his pecs and her pert little buttocks were rising and falling on him. As she descended, he was thrusting up, deep inside her. He was grunting in a low tone and she was sighing in a rich alto. I couldn't take my eyes off her. I wanted her riding me like she was riding Talal. But I wanted him too. I wanted to be on my back, with him riding my cock the way Emilee was riding his. When I couldn't take the tension anymore I stole back to my cabin and masturbated to a full and satisfying ejaculation.

I was so confused. I had already broken from Cape May and was riding the waves in the eastern Mediterranean. To a great extent, my choices had already been made for me. But was it all happening too fast?

I decided even before I reached Turkey that I'd reverse in my progression to the other side—for at least a while—and take it slower until I figured out what I really wanted from a changed lifestyle. The sex in Rome had been good—the sex had been terrific. But I can't say that it had fully satisfied me. There still was something missing. Until I figured out what that was, I decided I'd be more reserved. I'd concentrate on renovating my properties, opening my B&B, and becoming settled in a culture that was strange to me. And I'd have to figure out how my interests in photography and male nudes— and male-on-male copulation—fit into that. I still, thanks to international communications, could continue the side business I had set up for that. But how would the Turks feel about that?

Peter had said that for the right accommodations—meaning money—I would have no trouble with anything I wanted to do, citing the Turkish lawyer and Realtor he was sending me to, Cemil Teke, who openly lived under conditions that would slap him in prison in the States and that, by law, should do so in Turkey as well.

That's what Peter had told me about Teke, who certainly did seem to know how to grease palms to get my property purchased and renovations started even before I got there. Just as Peter had known how to take care of me royally in Rome, he seemed to be opening doors wide for me in Kusadasi, Turkey—maybe wider than I was prepared to walk through.

* * * *

The conditions on the wide concrete pier in the Kusadasi harbor were those of chaos. A cruise ship was in and berthed on one side of the pier and our freighter was on the other. A crowd of tourists was milling around on the pier and queuing up at various meeting points for excursions. Most of them would be going thirty-five miles into the interior to the ruins of Ephesus, which once was on the coast itself but had died as an inhabited city and busy ancient port when the river at the base of the mountain valley it had been built in silted up.

I had no idea where I was going. I owned a large old stone house somewhere up the slope in the old city from here and I had trunks on board the freighter that would be delivered there, but Peter had said that Cemil Teke was to arrange for me to be picked up at the pier and that a room and bath in the house I'd bought would be prepared for me.

I disembarked at the same time that the arousing couple did.

The woman had turned to me as she came down the freighter's gangplank and saw me standing there, small suitcase set on the ground between my legs as if I was protecting it from the mob that was swirling around me, and, fluttering her eyelashes at me, said, "Do you have a hotel to go to, Mr. . . . ?"

"Cliff. Cliff Strand," I answered.

36

"Emilee," she answered. "And this is Talal. He's familiar with Kusadasi. He's from Izmir, which is just down the coast from here. And I have a gift shop here—in the hotel district. If you don't have a hotel yet . . ."

If two people could look more eager than these two did that I not have a booking of my own to go to, they would be undressing me in public. Talal, young and trim, seemed to be fluttering his eyelashes at me too. At that moment I very much regretted that I hadn't made any move to hook up with one or both of them during the voyage.

"I'm very much sorry we didn't become better acquainted on the sail from Rome," Emilee said.

"Thank you, but I do have someplace to stay. I will be opening a small hotel here myself and my agent here has said a room there is ready for me."

"Ah, then, we will both be Westerners in the city," the young woman said, and the way she said it made me feel like we'd be clinging to each other—which, of course would be fine with me. "It's not a large city and the foreigners tend to stick together here. There's an English-speaking group that meets regularly here. Perhaps we will meet again here."

"Yes, perhaps," I said, but then I recalled that I supposedly had finished with women. My eyes turned to Talal.

"We would enjoy getting to know you better here in the city," Talal said. "*I* would enjoy getting to know you better," he added, and the look of interest he gave me was quite obvious. I couldn't help but return it, and thoughts of Emilee, naked, with me, receded into thoughts of me with Talal.

"I think I would like that too," I answered—truthfully—"I'm told the bed and breakfast I'm buying and renovating is on a street named Bozkurt Suk. Perhaps—"

"Ah, I know that street well," Talal answered.

Before I could say anything further or more specific about meeting, a beautiful young Turkish man—an older boy, I would more think—was there at my side, pulling on my forearm and saying, "You are Mr. Strand? I have been sent by Mr. Teke to guide you from the boat."

Giving a slight "what can you do?" smile to the two lovers who had fucked their way across the eastern

37

Mediterranean, but alas, without my participation, I picked up my suitcase, which the young man grabbed from me and started to weave his way through the crowd on the pier to dry land. There was little I could do other than set out after him, with a half worry that I had just been pick pocketed as I was told the people of all nationalities in the Mediterranean littoral states specialized in this.

We crossed the promenade avenue following the curve of the harbor, the young man ahead of me, weaving deftly through the crowd and me following with a good deal more brushing against shoulders and muttering of "Sorry" In English. I'd learned how to say that in Turkish, but, for the life of me, I couldn't bring up the word now.

On the other side of the street, a brick-floored central park-like area with café tables and trees spaced close together enough for their foliage to cover the area unfolded. On the three sides of the park away from the pier older brick, stone, or stucco buildings like I'd seen in almost any Mediterranean port town, if perhaps a bit more Oriental cast to them, with shops on the ground floors, enclosed the courtyard. Sitting at one of the tables was a mountain of a man flamboyantly dressed in yellow and orange, in Arab-style dress. A red fez, such as I'd see on a stereotyped Turk in a B movie, perched on his head. It was obvious that he was wearing makeup, and, as the lad running ahead with my suitcase, tended to evidence, I surmised that this was Cemil Teke, my new lawyer and palm greaser.

I was assured I was correct as I approached, as the man turned his hooded eyes and slight, knowing smile toward me, latched onto me, undressed me, assessed me, and settled down to some show of comfort and satisfaction that I couldn't gauge other than to get the impression that he found me acceptable and, I gave a little shudder, malleable. Peter had told me that there would be a condition of getting help from this Turk.

The young man got to him before I did, and I heard Teke say, "You may set that down here, Envir, and fetch us coffee." Suddenly I remembered enough Turkish to figure that out. As the young man scampered off, Teke turned his attention to me. He held out a bejeweled hand, but he didn't rise from the seat that he overflowed. I knew if he did stand, though, that he would tower over me. I took the hand—not being sure if I should have kissed it instead—and we didn't shake so much as Teke held my hand in his in a near-vice grip.

"Mr. Strand, is it?" he asked in elegant English. "Clifford Strand? Peter didn't tell me that you were a beautiful man."

What could I say to that? I ignored the last comment and simply said, "Are you Cemil Teke, then, the man who has so patiently guided me thus far in this brave—or foolish— Turkish adventure?"

"The same," he answered, "and I have thoroughly enjoyed being part of this transition. You have selected a fine property—in fact, three good—promising—properties. And we are making fine progress on your hotel. It lies just three streets up the hill from here. Still inside the old city. We will go up there after we have had coffee and chatted a bit. Ah, Envir is back with our coffee. Please sit."

I sat down beside Teke at the table and we chatted about my trip out from the States and our mutual acquaintance of Peter Phillips while the young man poured our coffee and then backed away from the table, sat down on the bricks on his haunches, and went blank. He was a fine looking young man, alabaster skin and jet black hair descending to his shoulders in curls. He was short of stature, but perfectly formed. There was no way, I thought, that he could have been of age. But from what Peter had told me of Cemil Teke . . .

"You know that when Peter was here, it was I who introduced him to Ergon Seljek?"

"Yes, he told me that."

"Ergon was a sweet young man. And a firecracker in bed. I enjoyed him for several years before passing him to Peter. I trust they are still doing well as a couple."

"Yes, they are devoted to each other," I answered. I did calculations in my head. Working from knowing Ergon was only twenty-four now, I decided that he must not have been any older than the young man here, Envir, when he was with Teke.

The young man was hunched down close enough to Teke that the lawyer absentmindedly reached out with one of his many-ringed hands and ran his fingers in Envir's hair as we talked.

"You must be tired from your trip," Teke said.

"No, I don't feel a bit tired," I answered. "Traveling by ship isn't nearly as taxing as flying."

"Ah, then, perhaps I can show you my bathhouse and you can be refreshed before we go up to your hotel . . . and there's the seal on the contract we can take care of from the beginning. I find in watching you approach from the ship that I have great interest in that."

I smiled wanly at him. Perhaps it was a mistake to not have arrived too tired to take care of that detail so soon. Peter had said that it would be decided in a wrestling match that I surely would lose, but Peter hadn't told me that Teke was a man and a half—whether or not he dressed androgynously and wore makeup.

As it was I didn't have a chance to answer directly, as Emilee and Talal were coming into the park at that point and Teke called them over and bade them sit with us. It was obvious that they knew each other. The conversation settled on how small the expatriate community was here.

"The English speakers gather every Tuesday night at a restaurant near your hotel, Clifford," Teke said. "The woman who owns it, Sheila Cantrell, is English. You must join the group."

"Yes, you must," Emilee agreed, putting her small hand on my forearm, squeezing it, and giving me a doe-eyed look.

Talal obviously saw the "fuck me" look, but showed no concern. "So, you're the mystery man who is refurbishing the big house on Bozkurt Suk for a boutique hotel," he said. "We'll be near neighbors then. We'll have to become better acquainted." He then was giving me a meaningful look, and I went hard. I'd seen both of them naked. I'd wanted both of them then. I wanted both of them now. Could it be I wasn't interested in switching all the way? That I was bisexual?

The two of them left and the conversation returned to the properties Teke had acquired and had begun renovating for me.

"I know you ran such a hotel in the States," he said. "And Peter tells me that a men-friendly hotel was being run beside yours and that you were interested in that."

"It was quite a busy operation," I answered.

"You could have such a busy operation with your hotel too," he said, "if you wished. We have not enough high-quality arrangements for men coming here with men and to be with men. There is a need for that here. If you wished to run such a hotel, I could help you stay in good stead with the law. I could also help steer business to you. You could give the hotel a Greek name. That's a joke among the Turks who are part of the man-love scene. Name something Greek and you are evoking Greek love—sex between two men. If you pointed to a man and said he was Greek, everyone will know that you were saying he went with men."

"It's something to consider," I said, not having considered it before. But it aroused me thinking about it. It would put me deeper in business with Teke, though, and I was finding him intimidating. At the moment I was finding him quite intimidating, as he had a beefy hand on my thigh and was squeezing.

"I think we should go to the bathhouse now," he said in a hoarse voice. "You have me hard. Go on up to the hotel now, Envir. We will be along shortly." Then he turned to me and said, "I am giving you Envir. You may fuck him if you wish. But I have set him up in the attic of your hotel and he will be your servant as long as you wish the arrangement. He won't cost you much."

I was lost on the "you have me hard" comment until Teke said what I could do with Envir.

"The age of consent here?" I asked.

"The same as where you came from—at least formally," he said. And then he laughed. "If we can bring Islamic law to Turkey, it will be twelve years old. We may progress to that in the not-too-distant future."

41

That needn't happen for me, I thought. But I said nothing.

We bathed at the bathhouse in a large pool where other men were reposing or moving about languidly in the water. A few of the men were engaged sexually with others, so I surmised that this was an "everything goes" bathhouse. Teke and I sat next to each other, and he checked me out under the water with a hand, but more like a doctor would than a lover.

We were massaged side by side after the pool, and I admit that I came to the masseur's intimate touch, but I was the only one of the four of us there who was embarrassed by that. The others treated it like it was natural, especially for someone uninitiated to this form of pastime as I was. Lying there, I watched Teke's masseur bring his massive cock to ejaculation as well. Teke watched me watch that.

The other three complimented me on my physique and conditioning, which helped me go hard and, eventually, to shoot off under the strokes of the young, muscular masseur. The two masseurs were built like Apollos. Teke was built like a whale, but was as muscular as the other two, and hung like a bull, and he carried himself like his was the most beautiful body there.

"The masseurs will go to the pool with us and you can use yours as you will. He says he would enjoy having you fuck him," Teke said.

This was too much too fast for me, though, and I said so. I was already building up nervousness over Teke's declaration that he would collect his initiation fee for services from me before we left the bathhouse.

Teke did take his masseur into the pool, though, and I sat beside him, hard and stroking myself, as Teke sat on the bench rimming the inside of the pool and pulled the masseur on and off his cock, as the young man sat in his lap, facing away from him.

Not long after that, it was my turn.

Teke was sporting. He said we could wrestle for domination, but of course it was no contest. We wrestled on a mat in a stone-walled room, with arched recesses and erotic frescoes on the walls of men wrestling and fucking. We wrestled naked, and Teke got on top of me and took the wind out of my sails with his weight and the power of his grips.

"Go up on your knees and spread your legs and it will be less painful," he whispered in my ear.

As he was working his cock inside my ass, I wondered how it possibly could be more painful. But eventually I opened totally to him and I went with his thrusts with counterthrusts of my own, concentrating on enjoying the fuck to the extent I could. I reached back and pulled my buttocks open, and I widened my stance and concentrated on being open for him, When I relaxed my body, didn't struggle, and let him have his way with me, I managed better. Still, this was enough to convince me that I much preferred to be the top.

Lying there, exhausted, on my back on the mat after he'd shot his load, I panted as he propped his head up with a bent elbow and looked down into my face. He was slow stroking my cock with his hand, and I knew he'd take me to climax.

"It's a pity that you are more a top than bottom," he said. "I sense that you are. You are very much like Peter was. You are more desirable than Peter was—for your age—you remind me quite a bit of an American movie star of some years back. But I can tell you prefer to be on top. You are older than I really like. I would have like to have met you twenty years ago. You know now what I can demand for easing your way through the systems here. This may be the last time, but maybe not. Until then, you may do as you will with Envir, and you undoubtedly will find your own men. Or they will find you. You will be a favorite for Turkish men who like to be topped."

I came for him and then he showed that that hadn't been the last time he would use me, as he rolled over on top of me, thankfully taking most of his weight on his knees pressed between my thighs. He palmed the small of my back with a beefy hand; commanded me to wrap my legs around his waist, pressing my heels into the flesh at the top of his buttocks, which I did; took the weight of his torso on his elbow pressed into the mat next to my chest; thrust inside me; and fucked the stuffing out of me—just as Peter had said he would do. This time I already was reamed open to his size, relaxed

43

immediately, moved my pelvis with his, and was able to get more enjoyment out of the fuck.

"Maybe this won't be the last time," he muttered, as we were cooling down from the second coupling.

After another session in the pool and being dried off and dressed by a couple of young Turks, we walked up to my new house, a stone mansion, set sideways to the street, of three stories, an out-of-ground basement, and an attic. I had been told that it was nearly 10,000 square feet of space, but I had had no idea what that looked like in real life. It was nearly twice as big as the B&B I was leaving in Cape May.

The lot was a big one, a double city lot, 60 feet wide and going to a depth of 150 feet. The house, 30 feet wide by 75 feet long, sat on the front, southern side of the lot. running along the northern wall to a parking lot at the back of the lot was a driveway. Between the house and the drive were a walled entry courtyard, with fountain, and a pool house, open to the back of the yard, where the hole being dug for a swimming pool surrounded by stone terraces lay between the house and the walled-off parking area.

The lowest of the three main floors had an entry hall on the front north side and a parlor running back from the front southern side. A balcony on the north side overlooked the courtyard half a story up. To the rear of that was an office area on the north, with a staircase on the south. A large dining room spanned the width of the back of the house. A balcony beyond that overlooked the pool, and there was a staircase alcove to the south side of the balcony that went down to the kitchen and storerooms under the dining room. The second and third stories were identical to each other, with three en suite bedrooms wrapping around from the front back toward the back, with a larger suite, with sitting room and bath, over the dining room. This made for eight guest rooms, each with a modernized bath, which was a luxury for Turkey. Until my village house in Bayraklidede was finished, though, I would occupy the third-floor, rear suite. The attic had an open terrace over the rear suite and, forward, a small flat and two servants' rooms, sharing a bath. The front of the basement area would be my photography studio and dark room.

44

Only the suite I was to occupy for a while had been completely renovated and the swimming pool wasn't more than a hole in the ground, but as I followed Cemil I could easily see how everything would work eventually, and I could tell that he had put a lot of effort into getting the renovations started. I wouldn't begrudge him his domination over me in the process nor fight him if he wanted more from me. I could see that I would need him for some time to come.

Envir prepared an evening meal and served it in the dining room, which was somewhat bedraggled but gave considerable promise of rising again. As I saw Cemil to the door, he reiterated that Envir was mine for the using. He made quite clear he had trained the young man to please another man sexually. Envir, in turn, would live in the attic in one of the servants' rooms and serve whatever needs I had for him at the hotel.

"And the English-speaking group," Cemil said. "It will be to your advantage to attend that and fit in with the expatriate community here. Remember, Sheila's Restaurant, just up the street, on Tuesday nights."

"I'll remember. Will you be there?"

"Of course. I can always improve my English." I nearly laughed. His English was better than mine—and more English. "And, about earlier. You are a desirable bottom, if you wish to go that way. You are too old for me, but there are several old, well-established men here, who would enjoy you, pay you well, and extend influence over you. I will help you find men you'd be pleased to fuck—some of them would pay an American like you well too and be of political advantage to you. Just tell me what you want. Incidentally, in case you are squeamish about that, Envir may look younger than eighteen, but he's passed that birthday. I probably wouldn't be giving him to you otherwise; I'd keep him for myself."

"For now, I just want to get my hotel and houses finished," I said, but I added my thanks for his other consideration. I knew it was politic to remain in his good stead. That led me to add to what I said. "Are there men, in either category, that you would want me to be with for either my or your advantage?"

45

"Perhaps," he answered, with a smile. "Just perhaps. And do think of specializing with this hotel."

"I will," I answered, already having decided to take up his suggestion.

As he was leaving, he pulled an official-looking document out of his briefcase and handed it to me. I assumed it was some sort of deed, but, as he showed by picking words out here and there and then a date, I discovered it wasn't.

I descended to the kitchen to wish Envir goodnight, and he gave me a look that indicated I would take him upstairs with me. But I didn't. I struggled with myself, but I didn't know what to trust, what to believe, and what I wanted. Cemil had sexed me up that day, though, and I was in a state. It did make a difference to me, though, that he was of age.

I locked the door to my suite, having resolved one thing, but I kept taking the document out and looking at it. When I heard Envir at the door, trying, unsuccessfully to open it, I put a pillow over my head and tried to ignore him at the door, knocking and calling out to me. When he was gone, I lay there, on my back, masturbating and trying, unsuccessfully, not to think of the birth certificate Cemil had handed me claiming that Envir, in fact, was of age or to think of the photograph of Envir, naked, Cemil had provided along with the question of wouldn't I like to use him as a model for my photographs?

Of course I would.

The door to his attic room was open and I could hear his heavy breathing and see that he was lying on his bed, naked, as I stood in the doorway, also naked. He was kneeling on the floor by the bed when I reached him and stood in front of him, gripping his hands in mine, as he made expert love to my cock.

I lay stretched out on top of him, him on his belly, his hands gripping the rungs of the brass headboard over his head, and one of my hands buried in the black curls at the back of his head and pulling his head up and back to me as I slid my cock inside his passage from above and fucked him and fucked him and fucked him.

* * * *

I woke up with Emilee crawling over me and stumbling out of bed.

"Sorry, it's late. I've got to get the shop opened. Have fun," I heard her say as if from a distance, through a wave of pain—my head, not my ass, so I assured myself that I wasn't the one who'd been fucked. I hadn't gotten drunk like I had the previous night during the English-speakers' gathering since my fraternity days at the University of Maryland. I registered in my pounding brain that from now on I'd forgo the 6.1 percent ABV Marmara Kirmizi beer and stick with the Efes Light. It had been Talal who had told me to try the Marmara Kirmizi. And it had been the sultry redhead Sheila Cantrell who had grinned, winked at me—she'd been signaling to me all evening—and asked me if I was sure when she plunked the second strong beer in front of me. And it had been Emilee who told me to chug it and then we'd walk home together.

I guess that meant I hadn't fucked Sheila the previous night—or her boyfriend, Alton. That had been my goal after I'd gotten half drunk. It seemed to have been their plan too— for me to stay around after the rest had left and the three of us having a go at it. Well, apparently it hadn't wound up being that three.

I hadn't realized that Emilee meant we'd walk to her flat above her souvenir shop, which was two blocks past my hotel-in-waiting, where Envir had assured me he'd been waiting from me in his garret room, on his back on his bed, naked and legs spread. I'd been in Kusadasi one day shy of a week and I'd spent every night on top of Envir doing pushups and the days wandering around in my developing hotel in a fog trying to stay out of the way of workmen, most, because of Cemil Teke's planning, being hunky young Turks sniffing around the rich, movie-star-handsome American Teke had suggested might become their sugar daddy if they played their cards right.

I'd gone to the Tuesday evening English-speaking gathering at Sheila's Restaurant as much to cool down and give my cock hard-on relief as anything, only to find Emilee and Talal there on the make for me and Sheila and her Turkish boy toy Alton Demir, as well. Cemil was there, sitting off to the

47

side, smiling, and no doubt amused by my total emersion in the sexual innuendo.

I'd found Envir a delight to fuck. He seemed so young and looked so innocent, but he was so expert. He knew how to work me and drain me totally in ways that almost scared me. Cemil had thrown him at me. There was little doubt that Cemil had spent considerable time training Envir before the young man had reached his majority. Cemil was throwing workers on the hotel at me too, and it wasn't clear that they all were of age. What was clear when Cemil was around was that he'd had them all.

Cemil had let me know that he would dominate me as he pleased. Who was running this adventure? Cemil or me? To what purpose? Was I paying for this hotel only for Cemil to ensnare me and, in the end, pull the rug out from underneath me—maybe see me put up on charges of one kind or another and taking my property for himself? Peter had told me that I had to watch the Turkish lawyer like a hawk. He'd told me that while, at the same time, telling me I had to trust someone in the corrupt system that was Turkish business and that it was Cemil Teke I'd need to trust.

But then, Peter had admitted that Cemil had dominated him too. And Cemil had said that he matched Peter to Ergon Seljek—who I'd recognized had Peter wrapped around his little finger and panting after him in bed. I doubted that Peter made any decision in faraway New Jersey that Ergon didn't agree with.

When I'd stumbled out of Sheila's Restaurant with Emilee and Talal, I'd known that I was going with them, not returning to the hotel and Envir's bed, and I'd told myself that it was a declaration of independence from the web Cemil was weaving around me. But he'd been sitting there and smiling while Emilee and Talal had been getting me drunk. So, was this according to Cemil's plans as well?

I reached out for Emilee as she rolled off the side of the bed, but I missed. I might have pulled myself off the bed and followed her, but Talal was awake now too and rolled over between my thighs, wrapping his arms around my thighs and taking my cock in his mouth. Most of the time we'd been working on Emilee in consort during the night, I had really wanted to be fucking Talal. The closest we'd come to intimacy beyond kissing and fondling each other was when I was on my back, my cock up Emilee's slit, as she rode my pelvis and Talal behind her, fucking her in the ass. It was my first time sharing a woman with another man. I was learning so much in such a short time in my journey to switching sides.

I'd felt him inside her ass while I was in her vagina, the membrane between her passages undulating at the coordinate stroking of our cocks inside her. I wanted to be inside Talal so much, though. And maybe I had been. But I could only pull in snatches of the three of us moving together.

I lay back on the bed, gripping the curly black hair of his head between my hands and reveling in the blow job. Turkish men—or at least the two I'd experienced so far—gave great head. I moved my pelvis and he readjusted to give me room to stroke up into his throat.

He didn't make me wait long, though. I had a huge, throbbing erection when he rose up over my body and lowered his ass onto the cock. I groaned deeply and grasped his waist as we moved together in the fuck, him saddled on my pelvis as Emilee had been last night, but this fuck, this fuck of a handsome young man, being so much more arousing than with any woman.

He rode me and rode me and rode me to a mutual explosion.

Only one week into my new life and I'd already exploded into hedonism. But was this free will or someone's sticky spider web?

~

Chapter Four: The Hotel Antinous

I lay, panting and spent, on my back on the mat in the fresco- and arch-walled stone chamber in the bathhouse in Kusadasi, my thighs spread, my knees bent, and my feet pressed into the mat to thrust my pelvis up to take the deep penetration of Cemil Teke's horse-hung cock as comfortably as possible. He was kneeling between my thighs, his knees pushed under my buttocks to elevate them, his fists buried on the mat on either side of my chest, his huge belly resting on mine, the jiggling movement of that mass of flesh having rubbed on my cock while he'd been thrusting inside me and having brought an ejaculation out of me and a laugh out of him.

I guess I had made the mistake of pleasing him too much when he exercised his contract option. He had summoned me to the bathhouse for a second wrestling match we both knew I wouldn't win—and I hadn't. But it was clear that I hadn't succumbed to his attempts to control me through the men he had put in my path over the last seven months in which the Hotel Antinous had come close to completion and my own village house in Bayraklidede was finished and I'd moved in. Moving in to my own house had even enabled me to wean myself away from Envir, who stayed back in the attic of the hotel as caretaker of the building and dining room waiter. What I had reached the need for was a reliable manager of the B&B.

It was the Hotel Antinous now—named for the only declared homosexual god, and named in Greek as a signal for those in the gay communities, where use of Greek was marked as gay by Turks, that the hotel encouraged gay male clientele. I had given in to Cemil—readily—on that point, and he had moved into a partnership of sorts with me, providing protection and clients in exchange for his domination and agreement for a good cut of the profits.

This, now, here—me on my back with him between my legs, his cock sunk deep inside me, was a reminder of his domination. He evidently found it necessary to reestablish that control directly after seven months because I had not succumbed to his attempts to control me through putting other men in my bed. He was reconfirming this control directly, himself. And I was panting under him, not a bottom by preference. But I had come for him—and he had come inside me and was still hard inside me, asserting control.

I struggled to roll out from underneath him, and he grabbed my wrists, forcing my arms over my head and my back flat on the mat under the weight of his belly. Although he'd come, he was still ramrod hard and so thick inside me that I felt I might split. The muscles of my passage walls were still undulating over the thick hardness of him, loving the attention even though, emotionally, I wasn't a bottom—at this moment no one had informed my channel walls of that. He reared back and gave me three hard, penetrating thrusts, and I lay quiet, panting, whimpering.

"I told you when you came here that you might need to give yourself to further your interests, our interests," he said when I was fully under control.

"Who?" I asked.

"The contractor, Haluk Badem," Cemil answered. "We need him to clear the way on the hotel occupancy permits. He wants you. He wants to use you as a bottom. If he's satisfied, once a week until the permits are granted. That could take a few months."

It could have been worse. Badem, who had done some work on the hotel, but mostly had worked on renovating my village house in Bayraklidede and virtually rebuilding the mountain retreat house in Kizlay Haber, which was more a ruin than a house, was ugly as sin. He was a good ten years older than I was. But he was built like a bodybuilder, muscular and strong. He was a regular gorilla. He had shown interest in me, and I thought that interest was genuine and an interest of his own rather than at Cemil's suggestion. Cemil had endeavored to pair me up with the younger workmen at the house, men who would let me fuck them. There was no hint with Badem of anyone doing the fucking but him.

"Say yes," Cemil commanded.

"Yes," I acquiesced. He pulled out of me then and moved away from me. "I will be in the pool in a half hour," he then said. "I want you to come to me there, walking the full length of the room, naked, and looking at me—and only at me. You will come to me in the pool, service my shaft, and then take it. Do you understand?"

"Yes," I answered meekly.

"Do you understand why?"

"Yes," I responded, knowing that he wanted the other men there to know that Cemil dominated the rich American who had come to Kusadasi to open a luxurious small hotel in the old town.

"My old friend, Umut Uzan, will be in the pool too. I owe him a favor, and he is in a position to make business life on Bozkurt Suk difficult or easy."

"I understand," I answered.

As I walked across the tiled floor alongside the pool, the pool being particularly crowded that day, I kept my eyes trained on Cemil, who was sitting on the lip of the pool, thighs spread, raging erection in his hand. I entered the pool at the other end and waded to him, men parting to let me pass as I proceeded, the hubbub in the pool having gone silent.

When I reached Cemil, I leaned over, he jutted his pelvis out of the water, and I took his cock in my mouth. There was buzz through the chamber, which accelerated as the older, fat merchant, Umut Uzan, took up position behind me. I grimaced as his hands squeezed and separated my buttocks and he split the difference with his cock. The buzz in the chamber continued as Uzan grabbed my hips and fucked me from behind as I sucked Cemil's cock. When Uzan was finished and had withdrawn, Cemil pulled me up into his lap, onto his shaft, and I crouched in his lap, my fists locked behind his neck, and my feet on the tiles on either side of his hips, giving me leverage to fuck myself on his cock. For all at the pool to see.

Cemil Teke had made his point not only to me but to the whole segment of Kusadasi men who went with men.

∗ ∗ ∗ ∗

For the next two weeks I was nervous around the contractor, Haluk Badem, waiting for him to start calling in the favor Cemil was giving him for his help in pushing the hotel to approval. In those two weeks, in which the hotel was shaping up into something really first rate, Badem was there, by my side, frequently, although he was spending more time up at the Kizlay Haber mountain cottage than at the hotel now. He was nothing but polite to me, although I occasionally was aware of him smiling at me in a knowing way.

When it came, I almost didn't realize it. He approached me one afternoon and said, "Would you like to come up to Kizlay Haber and see what progress has been made? There hasn't been much, but if you want walls removed or put in, this would be the time to do that."

"Yes, that would be fine," I answered. The village house up there, bought as a rambling stone ruin, was to be made into a vacation retreat triplex. The Hotel Antinous was more for foreign visitors coming to explore the ruins at Ephesus. Kizlay Haber was for Turks—gay couples, now that Cemil had led me in that direction, who were from Turkish cities and wanted to escape to the mountains on a vacation where they could lay back and freely be what they were.

As Badem's Land Rover climbed into the mountainous area above Kusadasi, he began to feel me out on whether I knew what Cemil had agreed with him and if I agreed to that myself. "Interesting name for a hotel," he said. "Antinous. That's a Greek name, isn't it?"

"Yes, Antinous was a Greek god," I answered. "But Antinous began life as a human and was born in Bithynia, which is now in Turkey. So the name is fitting for Turkey, I think."

"You know what a certain kind of Turk thinks of when a Greek name is used?" he asked.

"Yes. That's why we named the hotel what we did. Cemil has convinced me that there is profit to be made in a guest hotel in Kusadasi that caters to men who go with men. The name signals that. Antinous, as a human, was the lover of the Greek emperor Hadrian. He was made into a deity after he died."

Badem was silent for several moments and then he spoke again. "I understand that you are such a man—a man who goes with men. Cemil Teke has told me this."

"Yes, yes I am," I answered. "Cemil tells me you are such a man too. He tells me he has made an agreement with you for help in obtaining permits to get the hotel open."

"Cemil tells me that you usually do the, how do you say? . . . penetration. But that you will let me penetrate you."

"Yes," I answered, quietly, looking away from him and out of the passenger window. We were almost to the top of the terrain now. The land was arid, the trees gnarled from the whipping of the wind at this height. I'd been told that Kizlay Haber was in a depression between two ridges, with a brook running through it—that it was like an oasis, with lush vegetation, compared to the surrounding heights.

"That excites me," he said in a hoarse voice. "You have been penetrated before?"

"Yes. I just prefer it the other way."

"But you will give me good sport with me inside you?"

"I will do what I need to do to obtain those permits." I didn't feel the need to make him think I was overly enthusiastic about this.

"I will enjoy taking a man who takes other men. And you are a fine-looking man. A good body. And an American. That is a fetish with Turkish men—going with an American—penetrating an American. I will be forceful."

"Yes, Cemil told me you would be."

"We will struggle for it. If you win, you may choose to penetrate me or not to have sex at all. But when I penetrate you, you will want to scream. You will be bound and gagged, but I will not give mercy when you scream. Understand?"

"Yes. I won't win at wrestling, will I?" I asked, knowing the answer. He was a big, strong, heavily muscled man.

54

"No, you will not win. I was the champion wrestler of my village."

And I didn't win. I had no idea when we reached the cottage in Kizlay Haber that he would fuck me there, that day, but, once I saw what he had been working on there, I wasn't surprised that he did. He had everything set up for it. The house was still in ruins, which some of the outer walls crumbling and pulled down nearly to the ground and the vegetation encroaching into what would be the living space of the stone walled, roofed, and floored house.

I almost laughed, though, when I saw what Badem had done with the house so far. He had completed one of the baths, which was very modern had a large, glass-fronted shower. And in the bedroom the bath opened off of, he had set a double, brass head and footboard bed frame in the center of the space, with white sheets on the mattress. The wall toward the interior had been completely covered with a mirror, allowing whatever was happening on the bed clearly to be observed. I wouldn't call it a room yet, though, as the outer wall was mostly crumbled down. The space beyond the exterior wall was an interior courtyard with a fountain. He somehow had gotten the fountain to work. A ceiling fan was going whomp, whomp, whomp overhead too. But the outside was encroaching on the interior. Vines with large, green, glossy leaves had slithered into the space along the ceiling and down the walls. A section of the roof was missing, and for the time I was on my back, I could look up at an angle into the dimming light of the late afternoon sky as Badem hovered over me and worked my passage with his cock.

We wrestled on the bed, both naked, Badem heavy of body, muscular and hirsute, covered with black curly hair. He toyed with me, controlling his strength to be just a bit more powerful than mine, while holding himself in reserve, manipulating me until I was so exhausted that I just lay there on my back when we reached the point of him binding my wrists to the headboard and my ankles to the footboard. He gave me the handicap of detracting much of his attention to watching us in the mirrored wall, but even being given that edge didn't save me. By that time I already was open to him, as, in the process of wrestling, he'd had his fingers and his cock inside my channel from time to time.

When I was totally exhausted and had collapsed back onto the mattress, he already was inside me and it wasn't a scouting excursion at this point. I had the energy to spread my legs, bend my knees, and leverage my feet on the surface of the bed to provide the most comfortable angle for him to dig thick and deep inside me, as he reached up and bound my wrists to the restraints he'd already installed on the headboard and forced the ball gag into my mouth.

"You have neighbors up here," he gave as an explanation. "Otherwise I would enjoy listening to you scream."

And scream I did, through the ball gag, as my passage fought to accommodate his thickness and the varied angles of his stroking as he fucked me that first time. After he'd come and rested, he turned me on my belly, bound my wrists to the footboard this time and my ankles to the corners of the footboard. He left enough give for me to go up onto my knees, and he crouched over my pelvis and fucked me doggie style in even more forceful strokes then he had the first time. He'd reversed me on the bed so that I was pointed at the mirrored wall and he could watch himself kneeling behind me, grasping my hips, and fucking me. He bade me to turn my face toward the wall so that he could watch my grimaces in the mirror, and I obeyed him.

With a grunt after he'd come, he rolled off me and unbound me. I turned onto my back and looked up through the opening in the ceiling, bringing my breath back into a calmer rhythm, as he padded off to the bathroom.

Cemil had told me that obtaining all the permits we'd need, especially in view of the delicateness of what our clientele would be, would be difficult even for Badem to do.

"He'll need to really want to do this," Cemil had said. I got the message.

I waited until I heard the shower going and then I hauled my weary bones out of the bed as well and padded in to him. I had his back to the wall and his legs in a bit of a crouch, and I rode him in front, my fists locked behind his neck and my feet pressed into the slippery tiles of the wall behind him and under the cascading water, as I used the muscles of my legs to fuck myself on his cock. He was impressed.

We fucked again on the bed. This time I was unbound, on my back, and he was between my legs. He thrust and I counterthrust, moaned deeply for him, opened my mouth to his tongue when he wanted that, and fixing my eyes on the waning light of the sky above the open roof.

"You sure you don't enjoy having men inside you more?" he asked, as he was driving me back down the mountain to Kusadasi. "You were very good."

"Usually I don't like to be the bottom, but you were special," I answered. I knew it was what he wanted to hear. It was a bit of a chore but endurable.

"Perhaps we could . . . again . . ."

"We'll see what other permits or other help we might need," I answered, putting it all back into perspective.

~

Chapter Five: Men of My Own

I was sore for several days after Haluk Badem fucked me. I had been aroused by the coupling, but it had made me want to fuck someone myself—not be fucked again like that anytime soon. Cemil kept throwing men at me, mostly young construction worker types. They certainly aroused me, but I was becoming more and more determined to slip out from underneath Cemil's control.

I needed a man of my own choosing.

Having overheard talk among the construction workers of dating sites on the Internet, I decided to try to go that route—and far enough afield that the men wouldn't have connections to Cemil. I had picked up enough Turkish by now to have a basic understanding of navigating the Internet in that language, but I was pleased to find gay male dating sites hosted in Turkey where English was an option for navigating and profile reading and to discover that Turkish men were eager to learn English, as it was the international language of business.

The kicker is that dating sites couldn't admit to be based in Turkey or they'd quickly be shut down. It took me a while to figure out that that was the case. The trick, I learned, was to go to what appeared—and largely was—a Lebanese gay male dating site. This included sections on Turkey and other countries in the region where gays were routinely suppressed and thus couldn't have gay dating sites of their own. There were codes on locations, the Turkish locales not being directly identified. Again, overhearing the construction workers talk about this clued me in. There were men from Kusadasi on the Lebanese site, notably a few of the construction workers working on my hotel. I bypassed these, though, and, having learned the code location for Izmir, I zeroed in on those listings. Izmir was a bigger city than Kusadasi and was on the coast some sixty miles north of Kusadasi. That was only forty miles from my house in Bayraklidede. It seemed, I thought, far enough away to be beyond Cemil's influence. I certainly did what I could to keep from him that I was shopping on the Internet.

The key here was that I sought a man of my own choosing.

Turkey was not a comfortable place to be gay. Prominent men like Cemil Teke could be flamboyantly gay and even indulge in his fetish for younger conquests—but only with continual risk and a lot of palms being greased or favors dispensed. For the rest, the lifestyle was there, but it had to be kept under wraps unless one had a protector. That was what Cemil did for the Hotel Antinous. He put together a network of protection within Kusadasi, but, in so doing, he established control over me.

Izmir was as open with the gay lifestyle as anywhere in Turkey. It was still a strong undercurrent—older men and younger men and boys—in Istanbul, but very much under the surface, in back-alley dens of iniquity where only the very well placed and very wealthy could play. There was some of that in Izmir too, but Izmir was the most cosmopolitan city in Turkey and, with a U.S. airbase near at hand, was open enough for gay men that there were a handful of gay bars and, as long as you had transport, there was a gay beach at some distance west along the peninsula from Izmir.

I found quite a good selection of seeking men from Izmir on the Internet. Most appeared to be rent-boys; many quite obviously were underage, which I was determined to stay away from. All were eager to hook up with an American, most saying that they wanted to to practice their English. I wasn't fooled; I knew they wanted to get at an American's money. They also probably thought these would be short hookups, mostly with U.S. Air Force personnel, who would be leaving Turkey after a short stint. I had been warned that many of those I'd meet on the Internet in these services were married, with children, and were just double dipping for extra cash.

I didn't have any trouble attracting attention. I had written a profile identifying myself as a photographer who would pay good money to photograph naked young men for international collectors. I wasn't shy in adding that I'd pay for sex as well. A key part of the "not shy" was that, by now, I'd set up my darkroom in the basement of the hotel and put in enough of the studio for it to be functional and, with the use of mirrors, I'd taken high-quality nude photos of myself. I posted the real me on the dating sites and started getting hits just moments later. I remembered to thank the good genes I'd inherited from my movie star parents.

After several misses and prolonged journeys to "I don't think so," I settled on a young man, who, if he'd posted a photo of the real him, was a handsome devil, who looked intelligent as well as sexy. His profile said he worked in a lawyer's office, was a college graduate in business administration, twenty-four—thus thirteen years my junior, worked out, and was a swimmer (both of which were evident from his photograph), and was unattached. He didn't boast of being greatly experienced—more the opposite, which made him more attractive to me. And he was honest and smart enough to say "perhaps" to the photographs, but only if he could be masked and if the photos only went to private collectors and ones who weren't located in the Mediterranean area.

We agreed on meeting one evening at the Ehli Keyif bar on 850 Sok in Izmir, a smaller, more intimate, and discreet gay bar—one he said the American flyers didn't often go to. He claimed he was thinking of me, as an American, and maybe not wanting to run into other Americans. I gave him props for being sensitive and, after so many near misses already, I'd put him up at the head of the list.

I went to Izmir and booked for two nights, the night before our meeting and the night of our meeting at the Antikhan Hotel, which, by nosing around and obliquely asking questions, I decided was the best I was going to get in Izmir in terms of small hotels that didn't take a close, critical look at who walked by the front desk and up the stairs to the hotel rooms. I spent the day looking around Izmir and, at 10:00 that evening I was sitting at the bar at the Ehli Keyif, nursing an Efes beer.

The young man stood me up.

* * * *

10:45 and no Jemal—that was the name he had given but, of course, it wasn't his real name, I was sure—and two beers. I pushed the glass away from me and prepared to rise from the barstool.

"Excuse me. Are you alone? May I buy you a beer?"

I turned and looked at the tall, thin man who had come up beside me at the bar. He'd been here when I arrived, sitting alone at a table. He wasn't young, maybe ten years older than I was. He stood ramrod tall, a good head taller than I was. Very distinguished looking, he was. An authority figure type. Or a professor. Certainly a professional man, handsome of face, with chiseled features, a fine head of salt and pepper hair, with more gray at the temples. He was dressed casually, in a silk shirt, khakis, and leather loafers, but expensively, the clothes obviously tailored to fit his body closely. The top two buttons of his shirt were open, revealing darker chest hair than on his head. I had already noticed that he clearly was comfortable drinking in a gay bar.

"I was just about to leave," I said. "I may have had enough beer." It didn't sound even to me that I wanted to leave. What I wanted was to lay someone, and I was pissed that Jemal hadn't shown.

"Do you have to go?" he said. "Perhaps you'd like to change to scotch—on me, of course. Two scotches, Sami, if you please." The last was spoken to the bartender, who immediately went into action and produced the tumblers of amber liquor, neat.

"Thank you," I said.

"You've been here for a while . . . American, are you? From the airbase? Were you meeting someone who hasn't turned up?"

A lot to unpack. I took a sip of the scotch. I was drinking the man's liquor now. I was obligated to talk to him for at least the duration of emptying the glass he'd caused to be filled. It didn't really seem like an obligation, though. I'd never been with an older man as a top. I'd never thought of it. I assume the older of the two would be the top, and I wasn't shopping for a top. I was intentionally striving for switching sides entirely now—being the top with a man. Just another man and me. And I realized at this moment that I really was looking for a more permanent arrangement too. A partner.

"Yes, it looks like he isn't showing up," I said. "And, yes, I'm an American. But I'm not in the service. I'm a permanent resident in Turkey now."

"You said 'he.' So, you are aware of what kind of bar this is."

"Yes, although this is the first time I've been here."

"And the first time you were meeting with this 'he'?"

"Yes." I felt his hand on my thigh, and I turned and looked into his eyes. They were gray, searching. He seemed to know exactly what he was doing, what he wanted. I felt weak, under his control. I wasn't looking to bottoming for anyone.

"You were hooking up with this man?" he asked. "Sami, refresh our drinks, please." He turned his attention back to me and said, "So, you are Greek?"

That caused me to pause, and I almost repeated that I was an American, but then, thinking back on what I'd been told Turks called men who were gay, I realized what he was asking me. He wasn't asking me for a nationality now. He was being much more intimate—which went with that hand he had on my leg and that I hadn't shirked away from."Yes, I prefer men. I used an Internet dating service, but I guess the young man got cold feet." His hand had moved around to the front of my thigh, high up. His forefinger was pressing into the crease where my leg met my groin. It was like that was some sort of arousal spot, and I certainly was aroused by the pressure of the finger.

"Ah, a young man. And who was to be submissive? Him or you?"

"Him," I said, taking a long sip on the scotch. I'd have to stay at least until I'd finished the drink. But I knew I wanted to stay anyway. But did he want to? Was telling him I wanted to top putting him off? "I have been versatile before, but I'm here because I want to top." There, I'd said it.

He smiled, muttered, "Good," and his hand went to my crotch, cupping my package. "Is this OK with you?" he asked. "Are you nervous? Am I being too forward?" He was running his fingers down the sides of my engorging cock inside the material of my trousers. "Umm, nice," he murmured.

"No, I don't mind. I only want to top, though," I repeated. I both heard and felt my zipper being lowered. Then I felt his fingers searching for and finding the flesh of my cock. "Fuck," I murmured.

"Nice, very nice," he said. "I'll pay you 300 lira to let me suck you; 1,000 lira for the use of your body for the night. For the use of your cock—inside me."

"I'm not a rent-boy . . . not a prostitute," I said. He was fully encasing my cock and squeezing it. The lighting was such in the bar and we were turned so that no one could see that he was stroking me off right there. The bartender was nearby, but this presumably wasn't disturbing him even if he could guess what was happening.

"All the better. But perhaps you could be a rent-boy just for the night. I would use your cock, although I would not be submissive to you. I will take you inside me, but I will control. Have you ever covered a man who was dominant?"

"No."

"Would you like to have the experience?"

I gave that thought. Why not? "Yes, but you need not pay for it. You've spotted me two scotches."

"I want to pay for it. I want you to be prostituted to me."

"My hotel is . . ."

"I have a club nearby. From here I give the direction. You give me your body, your cock, for the night. But I pay and I command. You will be my prostitute for the night. From here, you do what I tell you to do, me using your cock."

His club was down a nondescript alley, but once inside the courtyard, all was opulent—and male. Two sides of the open-air courtyard were devoted, in two balconied stories, to rooms that opened out onto the passageway. The third side were the rooms of some sort of club, where, through the lighted windows, I could see men and I could hear music. But we didn't go there. We climbed the stairs to the second level of rooms opening off the balcony, he unlocked one of the doors and then locked it behind me again when I was inside. The room was like a movie rendition of a harem chamber: Turkish carpets on the floor and walls, a king-sized divan, covered in crimson silk taking up much of the floor, a modern bath off to the side, and silken pillows everywhere.

I lay back, swathed in pillows, on the bed, naked, while he knelt between my spread thighs and played with my cock with his hands until I was throbbing and panting. He too was naked and gaunt, but hard-muscled, ropey, his veins standing out blue on dark skin because there was no fat for them to run through. The hair on his chest descended in tight curls, getting ever darker down to his bush. His cock was long and thin, his balls hanging low. I was as long as he was but thicker and my balls nestled closer into my scrotum—at least until he started working on them, distending them, squeezing them, and rolling them, making me whimper and groan.

He played with my cock and balls for a good fifteen minutes. When I thought I might come, he slapped it, which caused it to lose its erection. He played it again to throbbing erection and then slapped it to half hard again, me moaning my frustration. At length He rose up my body, stretching out beside me, taking my mouth in his, invading my mouth cavity with his tongue, and taking my hand to his cock. We slow stroked each other to ejaculations, him taking me all the way this time, and then lay there in each other's arms, recovering our breathing.

"All night?" he whispered.

"Yes, all night," I murmured.

We lay there, fondling each other, letting our hands roam over each other's bodies. He was older than I was, but there was no downside to that. He was hard as a rock, handsome, and experienced.

He reversed on my body, hovering over me, and we sixty-nined each other to another ejaculation.

Later I was inside him, but he was doing the fucking. I was on my back and he was saddled on my pelvis, rising and falling on my cock, taking me deep, pumping himself on me with a vigor and for a duration I wouldn't have thought possible for a man his age. He was in better shape and was far more athletic than I was. A military man perhaps?

We slept, but sometime before dawn, I opened my eyes to see that he was stretched out beside me, his eyes watching me. "Something special before you leave?" he asked.

"Yes, please," I answered.

Again I was stretched out on my back. He was reversed on me, his legs encasing and squeezing my sides, his toes dug into the mattress, his fists gripping my ankles, while, my cock up his ass, he leverage on his toes, pulling on and off my cock. I came in an explosion and he laughed.

As the morning light shown through the window, we sat, yoga style, facing each other, our legs wrapped around each other's waists, our arms around each other's chests, with him providing the rocking motion, my cock deep up into his passage.

"My name is Onur," he said. "Do you live in Izmir?"

"No. I live in a village called Bayraklidede," I answered. "My name is Cliff." I didn't even think of giving him a false name. He was so much in control that I knew he had given me his real given name.

"I know where that is. You will come to me again? Maybe once a month? You will give me your cell phone number, and I will call to make arrangements. I will give you a key to this room and arrange your entry to the club."

"Yes. But the money . . . I don't . . ."

"You will be paid. You will be a whore—my whore. When you are here you will be a rent-boy under my full command. That will pleasure me, and I think the thought of being someone's whore might be arousing to you too. I will use your body—your cock—for money. This is important to me. This is part of my arousal in this arrangement. Everything else in my life is so proper. And I want this to be sordid . . . something different and just a little bit risky."

With that, I became a Turkish prostitute. And I learned how one could dominate from the position of a bottom. It was sex in which I was the top. I was moving closer toward a total switch from my earlier life. It wasn't a partner relationship, but it got me off.

He was right. I was aroused by the sense of being his whore. That was something that had aroused me in the way Cemil Teke used me too, but I only now realized what the attraction of that was.

* * * *

I left Onur's club purring and ravenously hungry. I was able to find my hotel and stopped at an outdoor café on the street below and ate a hearty breakfast. When I returned to my room, I opened up my e-mails on my laptop. There was an e-mail from Jemal, the young man I had come here to meet. My hand hovered over it, wondering if I should even bother to open it. If he had a reason for not meeting me the night before, he could have just phoned me, I thought. Then I laughed. I hadn't given him my cell phone number—nor had I asked for one from him.

"Sorry I did not make it," his e-mail said. "The bus from my village broke down. I am in Izmir now, though. If you still want to meet."

The bus from his village? He hadn't noted before that he wasn't from Izmir. But, then, although I'd told him in e-mail exchanges I wasn't in Izmir, I hadn't told him where I was from. Did I want to meet with him now? I had Onur now—or maybe I had him. But not more than once a month. He, as good as the sex was, was dominant, even from the bottom position. He was a little scary. And he was older. I had envisioned a young man, one who would be submissive to me.

"I have to check out of my hotel at eleven, unless I have a reason not to," I keyed. "If you call me on my cell phone before then and want to meet, we can meet." I keyed in my cell phone number. He called less than ten minutes later. I gave him the name of the café downstairs where I'd had breakfast and asked him when he could be there. He answered that he'd be there in less than a half hour. It was not quite 10:00 a.m. I stopped at the reception desk on my way out and extended my stay for another night.

I knew exactly who he was as he approached from down the street. He was scanning those sitting at the café, and after sweeping his eyes over me, his attention returned and focused on me. His eyes flared and he smiled. I guess I'd passed first-impression muster with him. He did with me, as well. He was in his mid twenties, was Lord Byron handsome, with alabaster skin; black, curly hair; hooded, bedroom eyes; and full, sensuous lips. His tight T-shirt revealed a good, if not overbuilt, physique. He was shorter than I was and trimmer. His linen trousers were baggy and thus didn't reveal much. He wore sandals without socks, and I found the shapeliness of his bare feet arousing. There was a shyness about him that promised submissiveness. There was nothing, on initial impression not to like.

He was also looking properly sheepish and apologetic. I accepted that he appreciated that he'd had an appointment that was his responsibility to keep and he hadn't done so.

"John?" he said, as he approached my table.

"Please sit down," I said, and he did so, across from me. I wanted to dominate and thought back to how easily Onur had accomplished that with me. I emulated the directness and command of the man I'd just been with. I could tell the young man was keyed up, but he didn't slouch in his chair, he leaned forward, toward me on the table, on his elbows and gave me a direct, apologetic look.

"I'm sorry about last night," he said. "I live in a village up near Ephesus—Seluk. There's bus service down here to Izmir. But my bus broke down."

His English was quite good; his apology seemed genuine. He wasn't the least bit cocky and his response to my direction had been submissive.

"You didn't tell me you didn't live in Izmir. And your name isn't Jemal either, is it?" For some reason I needed something more direct from him. His story was plausible, but he might just have had a better offer last night. He claimed to be new to this, but I wasn't sure of that now either.

"No, sorry," he said. I could sense a hint of desperation in him. He wanted to make this work. "My name is Serhan. Serhan Macar."

67

"And are you really a college graduate? And is there really a lawyer to work for up there in . . ."

"Seluk."

"In Seluk? You don't make enough up there that you don't have to come down to make money in Izmir from letting men fuck you?" I could believe from his excellent English and his demeanor that he was a college graduate, though.

"Yes, I went to college. I have a teachers' certificate. That's what I do in Seluk. I teach in a school. And that's why I said I was from Izmir and wanted to meet here . . . because I teach children in a school. And I am just beginning at this. And I have to go far from Seluk if I am going to be meeting with men. Teachers make almost nothing. I want a car—so I won't have to worry about the bus to Izmir breaking down."

We both laughed at that. It had broken the ice.

"And, so you will lay with me for 300 lira an hour?" I asked.

"Yes, if you have the place."

"For as many hours as I want?"

He hesitated on that, but then said, "Yes. If you don't beat me."

I didn't beat him in my hotel room, but I fucked him into the afternoon, and he stayed with me, responding to and submitting to all of the positions I put him into.

He stripped and let me take photos of him in provocative poses first. That had been part of the deal and he'd said he didn't care as long as it was covered in the pay-for-time coverage and the photos would be for private collectors far from here. I was careful not to photograph his face. To make it fair, I stripped down while I was taking the photos and we did some fooling around between photos, so we were both in heat and hard by the time I put the camera aside, sat on the edge of the bed, spread my thighs, and ran my hands into the curls of the hair on his head as he sank between my knees and took my cock in his mouth.

When we got to the fuck—to the fucks—he was quite willing and malleable and showed that he knew what he was doing. I was pleased to discover that the armoire at the side of the bed had a large mirror on the inner surface of its door. I didn't have to adjust the position of the bed much to have the mirror centered on the bed. I got more use of my camera, and Serhan went with the flow. I'd brought a tripod and a lead with a clicker on it, and I was able to position the camera in each position that I took the young man in and photographed in a way that neither the camera nor his face showed.

I played for the interesting poses. I placed him in a missionary position, with Serhan on his back, head toward the armoire, legs raised and spread, and me hunched over him between his flared legs, my fists in the mattress on either side of his chest, and pounding his ass. Then I turned him in place and fucked him doggie style, with him looking up into the camera, a gaze of pained pleasure on his face as I took him from behind. My favorite pose was of Serhan kneeling, upright, on the bed, facing the mirror, and leaning back into me as I knelt and covered him from behind, holding him close into my chest, kissing him as he turned his face toward mine, and with one arm embracing his chest and the hand of the other one stroking him off in the rhythm of the fuck.

Later, as we moved into the early afternoon, we slept, entwined in each other's embrace, both exhausted, but I woke before he did, gingerly rose from the bed, and snapped off more stills of Serhan in post-coital repose. I respected his request not to show his face, though.

I took him back down to the café for a late lunch. We were both ravenous from the energetic exercise we had gotten.

"What do you think?" he looked across the table at me and asked after we'd ordered.

"What do I think about what?"

"Was that it? Was that all?" I'd paid him 1,000 lira before we'd come down to the café. I wanted him to be assured that he'd be paid. He might have taken that as the final settling, I then realized.

"It can be all we do if that's what you want," I answered. "But I would like to continue it longer today. And I would like to see you again, if . . ." I was holding my breath. I really liked him, and not just because he was a great lay. I thought I might be able to have feelings for him.

"Yes, I'd like that," he answered. And I was able to let my breath out.

"This afternoon, I thought we might go to the beach. I'm told that there are beaches at the end of the Cesme Peninsula . . . that a beach out there was available to nude bathing . . . to gays."

"That's a long way away," he said. "It would take at least an hour by car."

"I have a car."

"I'm not sure we could return to Izmir early enough for me to catch the last bus to Seluk. I must teach at the school tomorrow."

"I could drive you to Seluk. I live in a village not far from Kusadasi. You would be almost on my way to my own home. And the next time we meet, I could pick you up and take you to Kizlay Haber. I have a place there where we could have privacy."

"The next time," Serhan said, giving me a dreamy smile. "That sounds so inviting."

There were a few men on the Cesme beach—couples mostly—but a few young, muscular men cruising the beach, looking for hookups. I was stretched over Serhan's body, on a towel, fucking him when one of these men came over, crouched down beside us, and watched. I had taken photos of Serhan, naked, coming out of the surf, before we fucked, and that had caught the young Turkish stud's attention as well.

This time Serhan volunteered that the photos could include his face.

Serhan had said it would be OK if I took photos of the other Turkish guy fucking him if it was OK with me, and so I got more good photos for my portfolio of the stud fucking Serhan on the towel after I'd done so.

Serhan was a perfect submissive. He did whatever I asked him to do and he was a beautiful young man. I wanted to do everything with and to him.

I now had two men of my own, men I hadn't hooked up with through Cemil Teke and thus always have the fear that the flamboyant lawyer was manipulating and controlling me.

70

Life would be good. I could feel it. I almost felt content
. . . almost. There still, though, was something inside me that
yearned for what I saw the Gaylords Inn owners, Alex Renard
and Sean Temple and Peter Phillips and Ergon Seljek as well,
had back in Cape May—a full partnership. Something more
than an occasional getting myself off with another man, no
matter how arousing Haluk Badem and Serhan Macar were,
each in his own way.

~

Chapter Six: Settling Down to Reality

I was bent over the side of the bed in the third-floor suite of the Hotel Antinous, arms stretched above my head, gripping fist-loads of bedspread to hold myself steady in position, watching the flamboyantly dressed Cemil Teke lounging in the sitting area across the room and viewing me being fucked hard through hooded eyes. The big, rough, Turkish seaman and smuggler was saddled behind me, grasping my hips in his rough hands, and fucking me hard. He'd been rough enough that I had cried out at his first, cruel penetration. I'm sure that my cries had rumbled through the halls of the hotel, where every room was occupied now, merely nine months after the hotel had opened. But, as men were undoubtedly being fucked all over the premises at the same time the man Cemil had brought to me was dominating me, my cries had just blended in.

We were running a full-scale male brothel here apparently, and Cemil had gained nearly total control. I had become just another male prostitute to Cemil's intricate networking to support his journey ever deeper into illegal and illicit activities in Turkey.

The man he'd brought to me was yet another piece in the puzzle Cemil was putting together to feather his nest. As an American, who kept myself in shape, I was a valuable chit in Cemil's game of exchanging favor for favor. He didn't call upon me often—and then only when the stakes were high—but he didn't take my wishes into consideration when he did.

The big bruiser pulled out of me and hauled me up onto the bed, on my back, stuffing a pillow under the small of my back as he did to elevate my pelvis. I tried to rise and he backhanded me across the mouth, drawing blood. I lay back and docilely spread and legs and bent my knees, opening to his cruel thrusts inside me as he hovered over me between my legs. His hands went to my throat, and he was choking me as he thrusted again and again, not particularly long or thick, but cruel and powerful in his thrusts. My hands went to his wrists, trying to dislodge his grip on my throat, but to no avail. He was too strong for me. I blacked out.

When I came to, the smuggler and Cemil were across the room, sitting in tub chairs and discussing their business in low tones.

"I will supply all of your needs for those booked at the hotel at low prices," the smuggler was saying. "But I want a place for storage as well, to support distribution throughout the region."

"We can manage that," Cemil replied. "We want more than the drugs, though. We want liquor and cigarettes at cheap prices too."

I didn't need to hear more than that to know what Cemil was dragging us—me—into.

The smuggler had seen that I had come to, though, and was moving back to the bed, his manhood, such as it was, hard again, cruelly curved up. I tried to roll off the bed, away from him, but he was too fast and strong for me. He fucked me stretched out on top of me, my belly to the bed. I reached up and grabbed the rungs of the headboard over my head, and he grasped my wrists with his fists, holding me there, while he fucked me from behind and above with hard strokes.

After they left and I had showered, I took my lunch in the dining room. There were three other couples, all male, having their lunch, all absorbed in each other. Envir, who was waitering today, brought me an Izmir newspaper, which I perused as I was waiting from my food to arrive and mulling at the back of my mind what I possibly could do to keep the hotel from sinking deeper into crime by becoming a distribution center for illicit substances.

I stopped on page two, the trembling in my hands almost preventing me from making out the words in the caption under a photo there. The photo was of some sort of ribbon-cutting ceremony. My periodic, authoritarian older lover in Izmir, Onur, was in the photograph. He was identified as Onur Sadik, police chief over the entire Izmir region, which stretched down to Kusadasi. The man I was fucking once a month, but who dominated me as we fucked, was no less than the top policeman in the region.

"What do you see that makes you smile so?" Envir said, as he poured water in my glass.

"It's nothing, Envir," I said. But just maybe it was everything, I was thinking.

* * * *

Moving my hips back, I pulled out of Serhan's ass, but I remained holding him to me in a chest-embracing hug where I'd held him as I took him in a side split. We were on the iron bed in the bedroom of the one of the Kizlay Haber mountain village stone sections of the triplex I'd had rebuilt. The units were in high demand, but I'd kept one—the one where the contractor, Haluk Badem, had fucked me when only the bathroom had been built—for my frequent trysts with Serhan. He continued to be a sweet and compliant lay. He'd given it all to me this afternoon even though I knew that he was devastated.

The room was much the same as it had been when Badem brought me here and royally fucked me. He'd wanted to do that again after that, but I'd held him off. I was weaning myself away from being used as a bottom in my quest to totally switch sides from a husband of a woman to an exclusive top for men. Only Cemil Teke now was able to pull me back into the role of bottom and only then for other men he was trying to strike deals with and who wanted me to be part of the deal.

Although the room looked mostly the same when it had been in ruins, it wasn't. Badem's reconstruction of the stone triplex was complete, and he'd done a great job. This room, though, I'd wanted to leave to appear much as it did the first time I saw it. The wall to the small courtyard, the fountain now functioning, still was low and jagged topped, but what had once been open was glass, with a glass door to the courtyard.

The wall to the interior corridor still was one large mirror. Openings at the top had been left to accommodate the vines that still invaded the room. The opening in the roof had been replaced by a large, expensively irregular-shaped skylight. I'd left the bed in the center of the chamber, with no other furniture in the room. The bureau, armoire, and chair were in a dressing room leading to the already-modernized bathroom.

I wanted the focus of the room to be the sturdy iron bed with the pristine white sheeting, and, when possible, on the young man on the bed. I did have tripods and cameras spaced around the bed and light fixtures high up on the walls, providing lighting to highlight the bed.

I took photos of Serhan before, during, and after the fucks. I occasionally brought in guests from the Hotel Antinous who attracted me and who were willing, and photographed them fucking each other on the bed—and, occasionally one of them fucking Envir and sometimes, when he was willing, and he always seemed to be willing, Serhan, although increasingly, as my relationship deepened with Serhan, I kept him to myself. I didn't fuck or photograph myself with anyone there except Serhan. The photographs and videos sold very well on the Internet to my specialized clientele, and I was being made quite rich from this aspect of my business.

I told Cemil Teke as little as I could about the photography service. If he knew how well that business was doing, I'm sure he would have moved in on that as well as on the hotel business.

After quietly rising from the bed so as not to disturb Serhan in his doze, I padded around and turned off the video cameras that had been filming us and took one of the still cameras and moved around the bed, taking photos of the beautiful young man's debauched body. He couldn't lie in anything but a sexy pose if he had wanted to.

Then I went into the bathroom and showered.

When I came out of the bathroom, he was sitting up in bed, looking dejected but very, very desirable. I had been thinking of him and of his body and of the threat that I might be about to lose him if I didn't do something about his plight. I was in full erection again when I came into the bedroom. I went around and switched the video cameras back on. Moving to the bed, I sat on the side, and, with a shy smile and correctly reading my desire, Serhan crouched in front of me and took my cock in his mouth.

After a few minutes, I pulled him up, positioned his hole on the bulb of my cock, and pulled him down into my lap. The next fifteen minutes, with the cameras whirring, was spent with Serhan's torso arched back toward the floor, his arms stretched out on the stone floor and me pulling him on and off my cock with a strong grip on his hips. When he had come in an arc splashing back on his belly, I pulled him up and close into my chest and gave him my load.

We sat, rocking back and forth against each other. He was moaning slightly, but I knew he was still in a melancholy mood. He'd told me why after I'd picked him up in his village of Seluk for the drive over to Kizlay Haber.

"I will have to go back to Ankara," he had murmured, his voice sad.

"Ankara? That's far in the interior, isn't it? For a visit? You have family there?"

"Yes, that's where my family is," he'd answered. He'd already told me during an earlier tryst that his family lived far away. I'd asked because I'd been in the country long enough to know that the society here was very family oriented. The more family you had about you, the less likely you were to become involved in any activity like homosexuality. Serhan was very open and submissive with me. I wasn't surprised to hear that was because he was well away from the embrace of his family. "And, no, not for a visit. Forever."

A chill of consternation raced up my spine. "Forever? You can't . . . I don't want—"

"I have to leave Seluk," he said. "And I have to stop teaching there."

"Why?"

"I had been sleeping with the principal of my school— before I met you. He was cruel and he beat me, but he took care of my needs too. He has been exposed. It's only a matter of time before I am implicated in his sin. He was stoned and almost died before the police intervened. It will not go well

76

with him, though. Someone teaching children and sleeping with anyone they aren't married to, let alone one of their own kind. It's not tolerated here in Turkey. I don't want to be stoned."

"You'd be leaving soon?" I asked. My nerves where clutching. It was all I could do to keep the car on the road.

"If I were not meeting you today, I would already be gone," he answered. "They have the headmaster at the police station. I'm afraid he was telling them about the men he'd been with."

We hadn't had time to say more then; we'd reached the triplex in Kizlay Haber. And the threat of losing him had put me in high heat. We'd gone immediately to the bed.

Now, though, when we'd fucked for nearly two hours and both had come repeatedly, I knew what I wanted to say . . . to do. I'd had time in the shower to work it out . . . time enough that I knew it was a step I wanted to take, that last step to what I wanted in my switching sides lifestyle progression.

We were sitting in an embrace, me on the side of the bed, my cock still deeply embedded in Serhan's passage, and Serhan in my lap, his legs spread around me, bent, and his knees pressing into my sides. We were embracing each other's chest with our arms, and kissing.

"I'm not taking you back to Seluk," I murmured. "From what you've said, it might already be too dangerous for you there."

"But what can I—?"

"I will give you two choices. I'll buy you new clothes either way. Then I'll put you on a plane to Ankara if you really wish that. Or I will give you a job at my hotel at Kusadasi. You have a business education and I need someone to manage the reservations desk."

"A job? In Kusadasi? In your hotel?"

My emotions soared. He'd bypassed the Ankara choice that would have devastated me and went to contemplating working for me in Kusadasi. I could tell that he was pleased by the prospect—and I really did need someone I could trust to run the reception desk, someone not supplied by Cemil Teke.

"And there you have a choice too," said. "There's a small flat in the attic of the hotel you could have as your own . .

. or . . . you could live with me in the village of Bayraklidede." I was putting it all out on the line there. It was a serious step to take. Was I ready for it? Yes, I was. I was aching for a permanent relationship.

"Live with you, in Bayraklidede? Be with you? Be your . . . ?"

"You would be my partner . . . my life's partner," I answered, looking deep into his eyes to discern what he wanted. Had I gone too far, too fast? No, I could see that I hadn't.

We kissed deeply and then he pulled back from his embrace around my torso, pressed gently on my chest to signal that I was to lie back, which I did. Then, with me lying back on the bed and him saddled on my cock, Serhan reached down and gripped my waist between his hands and, using the leverage of his feet on the surface of the bed, started to rise and fall on my cock, fucking himself once more astride me . . . while around the room, the video cameras continued to whir, taking it all in.

* * * *

"Did you find something you liked in the paper?" Serhan asked. We were sitting at one of the tables in the dining room at the Hotel Antinous, and Envir was pouring us coffee. He could see that I nearly was grinning.

"Yes, very much, I said," and I showed him the article in the Izmir newspaper.

"Cemil Teke has been arrested?" he asked. "And that's good news? I thought—"

"Yes, that's very good news, Serhan," I answered.

"Won't we—?"

"No, we'll be fine. It's already taken care of."

And so it was. The regional police chief, Onur Sadik— my occasional lover who was obviously so taken with me that I barely needed to express my problem before he said he'd take care of it—and of me and my operations in Kusadasi—had proven to be more powerful than Cemil and all his friends combined were. A smuggler had been caught trying to bring drugs and contraband liquor and cigarettes ashore. Cemil Teke had been arrested as well. Both had been hauled off to Izmir and already were on their way to a prison in Ankara. Cemil was well away from here. And Onur had promised that neither I nor the Hotel Antinous would be connected with Cemil's activities even if Cemil tried to do so. But Cemil didn't know anything about my connection to Sadik. There would be no reason for him even to know that Sadik was involved in his apprehension and quick transport to Ankara. Teke had too many high-level connections for him to be seen or heard from in public again once he'd fallen from grace.

I had Onur well in hand. He hadn't asked anything of me other than continued monthly trips to his club in Izmir. I looked around. Serhan was here and enjoying his work at the hotel and doing very well at it. Ever the submissive, he also was doing well and appeared to be happy at our home in the seaside village of Bayraklidede. He continued to be tolerant of anything I desired. I wasn't asking him to film with other men anymore, but he wasn't asking me about who I went with other than him. I looked up at Envir, pouring our coffee and giving me a submissive look. I enjoyed him occasionally still.

I looked around the dining room. Three of the couples, two where both were young and muscular, and a sugar daddy and boy toy combination, had happily been filmed fucking in the studio downstairs. Couples booking here were starting to ask for that, as a service, with them getting copies of the DVDs.

Was I content now? Yes, I suppose so, now that Cemil Teke was out of the picture. For the first time I could tell myself I'd made it all the way. It had been a messy switching sides transition from heterosexual husband to what I had now. But it was, I thought, a worthwhile journey. I was a top now exclusively and I was sitting pretty—and well protected—with my businesses here in Turkey.

My sitting pretty lasted for about fifteen minutes.

"There's a telephone call for you," Envir approached the table and said.

I went to the office to take the call. It was Onur Sadik, from Izmir.

79

"I presume you've seen the newspaper article about Cemil Teke," he said.

"Yes, I have. Thank you."

"There is something you can do to thank me," he said, "and to earn my continued patronage."

"What?" I asked, a sense of dread seeping into my bones. This was Turkey. I'd learned what the meaning of "scratch my itch and I'll scratch yours" meant.

"There's an important member of parliament who visits Izmir occasionally. He is a special friend of mine, a member of my club, and he's heard about you."

"Yes, and?" I asked, knowing I didn't need to ask.

"You told me that you could be versatile if need be. With Ahmad, you need be. Do you understand?"

Of course I understood. So, it began again.

~

About the Author

Habu is one of the pen names of a former supersonic spy jet pilot, intelligence agent, male model, movie actor, and diplomat. A wild youth in Southeast Asia was spent enjoying whatever sexual opportunities came his way, and much of his gay male writing is about recalling incidents from those days and inventing ones he'd perhaps have liked to experience. He now leads a very quiet and ordinary happily married family life.

An American, he is a published mainstream novelist and short story writer under another name and in another dimension of his life. He has written or cowritten (with Sabb) approaching 1,000 published short stories and over 100 published erotica e-books, primarily of gay fiction but also memoir, straight fiction and ménage fiction. His hand and creative writing can be seen in stories and books by habu, sr71plt, Dirk Hessian, Shabbu, and Stephen Kessel—among unrevealed others that might surprise readers. The fictionalized GM memoir *Flying High, Diving Deep* is loosely based on his life experiences. He can be found at the adults only gay male site www.BarbarianSpy.com, which he shares with Sabb and Dirk Hessian.

Our authors always like to receive feedback, and appreciate it when readers post reviews at distributors and other sites.

BarbarianSpy

FOR LITERARY HEAT

BarbarianSpy Books

Not all books listed below may currently be on release.
* indicates the book is available in paperback and e-book.
BOOKS BY CHRIS CROSS
Multisexual Adult Romance
Pulaski Square
Chocolate in Vanilla (MF)2
Christmas with Chris (MMF) (MM) (MF)
BOOKS BY ALEX LOCKHEED
Transgender Romance
Meeting Jenna
Transgender Other
Being Sarah
BOOKS BY DIRK HESSIAN
Xtreme Historical Erotica
Dirk's Ancient Times Collection (Print only Bundle)*
The King's Men
Shores of Tripoli*
Prophecy of Noto
Pretender's Fate
General Historical Erotic Romance
Dirk's America's Founding Collection (Print only Bundle)*
Soldier,Spy
Ridden West
Deliver a Virgin
Clouds and Rain
Confederate Gold
Puttin on the Ritz
To the Hessian Hills
Fire Down the Valley*
Constantinople*
The Beautiful Way*
Blue and Gray
Colonel's Treasure
Beginning of Time
Labyrinth

Arena Stage
Trading Partners (Valentine's Day)
Four Coins
Lower Than the Heart (Valentine's Day)
Brambleton
Finding Amnad
Platres Conclave
Other Novels/Novellas
Also Want to Thank
Ranger Guided
Key Westing
Syrian Ram
Temptation's Clutches*
Descent into Chaos
Escape to Girne
Journey Through Abilene
Harmony and Dissonance
Stallion Station
Racing With the Devil (espionage suspense)
Prepared in Cape Verdi
Gilded Cage
House on Park*
Anything for Ambition
Dance of the Ravishers
Hard Knocks U*
My Neighbor's Spa*
Man's Man: Tales of a High Priced Gay Hooker*
Trip Money
The Indian Doctor
Sailorboy
Home to Fire Island
Switching Sides*
Murder Mysteries
Retribution (Hardesty)
Snitches (Hardesty
Gotta Keep Trying (Hardesty)
All Fools Day Foolery (Mike Kavanagh)
Inevitable Case (Mike Kavanagh)
Vanishing Laura
Death on a Ping Pong Table
Clint Folsom Mysteries Compendium Volume 1*
Death to Blonds - Stolen Judgment (Clint Folsom Mystery)*
Clint Folsom Mysteries Compendium Volume 2*
Gay Erotica Anthologies
A Hell of a War*
Earth Cry*

Shunga
Habu's Christmas Balls
Eight in D*
DevilMENt
Silas' Choices*
Stallion Station (A Novella in Parts)
Eleven to the Dogs*
Fifty Seventy*
Spy Tails 001*
Spy Tails 002*
Doubled*
Doubled Again*
Tails in the Tropics*
Tails in the Med*
Tails in the West*
Rough Riders*
Grab Bag 1*
Grab Bag 2*
Grab Bag 3*
Grab Bag 4*
Grab Bag 5*
Grab Bag 6*
Grab Bag 7*
Grab Bag 8*
Grab Bag 9*
Grab Bag 10*
Grab Bag 11*
Grab Bag 12*
Beyond the Beaded Curtain*
The Sporting Life*
Fetish Galore!*
Literary Gay Erotica
Cairo Surrender*
The Handyman*
Homeward Bound
Journey to Mirage*
Bisexual/Menage/Multisexual Erotica
And Eat it Too
Two Men, One Woman*
Every Which Way
Summer of Denial
Death on a Ping Pong Table
Cruising Gigolo
13 Ways for Halloween
Luther*
The Indian Prince*

85

BOOKS BY SABB
Spanish Lovers
Driver Reliever
Hiring in Hollywood
The Legend of Holleystone Grange
Surprise Encounters*
She is He
Wrong Man
Loyal to his King
Barbarian Tales - Book One - Traveler's Tales*
Barbarian Tales - Book Two - Journeys Begin*
Barbarian Tales - Book Three - The Inheritance*
Barbarian Tales - Book Four - Road to Persepolis*
BOOKS BY SHABBU
A Season in Galicia*
Blind Dates*
Velvet Interrogation
Finding Jason
Dirty Pool
Operation Black Jade
Cigars!*
Angel in the Barn
Gayly Complicated*
Despoiling David
The Tree of Idleness*
I Met a Man
Rough Road to Happiness
BOOKS BY STEPHEN KESSEL
Gay Romance
The Forever Man
Two Chances
BOOKS BY KIM BLACK
Lesbian Romance
Transfixed on Tammie (F/T lesbian)